After Tomorrow

by

Amy Gleason

Acknowledgements

People say writing is a journey. I believe that now that I have finished this book! It took me a long time to have the courage to let anyone read my original work, titled *Freundschaft*, and I am forever grateful to three very special friends – Becca, Kristy, and Brenda – whom I trusted with my first draft. You did not let me down! Your feedback gave me the confidence that I had something worth pursuing, and that was the serious beginning of this incredible journey!

When considering acknowledgments, I want to thank Abigail at BookBaby for being my "person" in the self-publishing industry. From that initial phone call, to the enthusiastic responses to every one of my emails, you've continually been a reassuring partner in making my dream happen. Thank you, Abigail, for all of your help!

Now that I'm officially published, I must give shout-outs to Janine, Darin, Tara, Deb, Caitlin, and all the others who took a chance on me with my debut novels *Freundschaft* and *Tanzen*. You looked past the German titles and cartoonish book covers, with faith that I had good stories on the pages in between. I have SO appreciated your support! Thank you to my daughters Shayla and Camryn, who secured me sales and a loyal teen audience before the books were even available. Shout-out to those teens – Margot, Cynthia, Chloe, Maddie, and Emerson – for proving that there is a market for my stories. And thank you to my superfans – Faryn, Rebecca F., and Rebecca U. Your relentless enthusiasm has added so much joy to my writing, and it is certainly motivation for me to continue the series!

I also want to acknowledge my wonderful husband, Ryan, who doesn't really "get" this writing thing, but has never squawked about all the time and money I have invested in my passion. I truly appreciate your love and support!

Finally, and most importantly, the biggest hug and shout-out goes to my sister, Kari, whose constructive editing came with blunt and witty feedback every step of the way. The assurance you gave me kept me moving forward, and that has meant the world to me.

Now, here we are! Enjoy!

After

Tomorrow

"Tomorrow is really just what's left of today. It's what's after tomorrow that you need to plan for, for that is your future."

-Mr. Charmin

ISBN: 979-8-9873858-5-2

This is a work of fiction. Any perceived correlation between this story and real-life events is coincidental.

*No, the main character is not me, and no, you are not in this book. ☺

www.amygleason.net

This book is self-published through Bookbaby.com (info & sales: store.bookbaby.com)

Genre: realistic fiction, young adult fiction

Table of Contents

Chapter 1: Upper Crusters

The first-hour warning bell punctured the chatter and commotion that flooded the hallways of Liberty High School, as students slammed their lockers shut and scuttled to their homerooms. It felt too early in the morning to be back on this first day after Winter Break, though the giant main hall clock confirmed the bell's accuracy.

The large timepiece, facetiously known as the *Big Ben* of Liberty High School, took up an entire wall at the end of the school's central student walkway. Sporting Roman numerals sized to the height of an average adult, *Big Ben* was a gift to the school from the Parent Teacher Organization a whole generation earlier. This gift came with the promise of punctuality for students, though occasionally the simple logistics of a schedule precluded that.

Spring semester of senior year had officially begun, which meant now the proverbial clock was really ticking for the students. There was only so much time left until "after tomorrow," a term that was coined by the school's English teacher.

"One often thinks of *tomorrow* as the future," Mr. Charmin had explained to his homeroom students, a captive audience, just before Winter Break. "But tomorrow is really just what's left of today. It's what's *after* tomorrow that you need to plan for, for *that* is your future."

Mr. Charmin was deemed wise for this viewpoint, which shifted the focus of his homeroom students in their senior year. Students were challenged to consider how the things that seemed monumental today would still affect them after tomorrow. He advised that some things were worth putting energy into, but other things could be let go.

"Tomorrow," then, was only a handful of months to maintain that GPA, commit to respectable post-secondary plans, and preserve the precious teenage friendships, that, for many, were as critical to survival as water and oxygen. There was also only so much time left inside "tomorrow" to appreciate the luxuries of living at home under the care of parents, with the nagging reminder that this time should also be used wisely to prepare for what Mr. Charmin claimed would come "after."

***

Joanna Conors slipped into her desk just as the first bell rang, and her homeroom teacher, Mr. Charmin, put on his cheaters. "Nathan, I'll have you take the desk behind Joanna," he said to the student standing near him, and he motioned to the back of the room.

Joanna looked up upon hearing her name, to see her tall, handsome classmate stroll confidently along the row of desks, passing her. Nathan Hooks took the only empty seat in the room. As was typical of young men experimenting with cologne, Nathan did not seem to understand that less is more. The room was engulfed by his Calvin Klein *Obsession for Men*.

While his scent was overpowering as he passed Joanna, it would soon become a welcome aroma. Nathan Hooks, a classmate for four years but who never once had an interaction with Joanna, was extremely attractive. His overuse of the cologne only added to the allure.

Mr. Charmin was very structured and kept a routine that most students took comfort in. One could predict that he would next clear his throat, welcome the group back from Winter Break, and then go through all the housekeeping items that teachers had to address during Homeroom.

But Joanna wasn't listening.

***

"So, what's the 411, girl?!" Phebe Schoeneck, Joanna's absolute best friend since kindergarten, demanded, as the two rushed through the crowded hallway to get to second hour. "He's in your homeroom now? Dish!" Phebe typically managed the headlines in their middle-class social circle, but this question came with a sincerity that only resided within their best-friendship.

"Yep, and he didn't say a word to me the entire hour," Joanna confirmed with a confidence that was smug, yet annoyed. "Didn't look at me when he passed me to get to his seat, and didn't talk to me at the end of the hour during our work time."

Phebe clutched her economics textbook to her chest and offered an explanation that was very matter-of-fact: "That's because we're not upper crusters."

"I'm surprised he even knew where to go when Mr. Charmin said *behind Joanna*. But, yeah. Whatever." Joanna rolled her eyes to dismiss the governing social order of Liberty High School.

"Oh, he knows who you are," Phebe assured her. "He's just not allowed to talk to you."

"You know, we're getting a little old for that, don't you think? I mean, seriously. We've all been together for four years now, and many of us since kindergarten. Can't we just all be friends?"

Phebe looked up to see the two upper crustiest of all the upper crusters, Pelin Yilmaz and Dana Strohbeck, walking towards them. The two pom squad captains stopped when they came to their teammates. "Don't forget, extra practice today after school!" Pelin announced with a fake smile. Her flowing black hair bounced around her shoulders after the abrupt halt to her pace.

The gorgeous Turkish girl, who was very fake-nice outside of practice, was definitely at the top of every guy's list of who they wanted to date. There really was no reason for Joanna not to like Pelin, other than that Joanna found Pelin's value system to be questionable. But Pelin was in the popular crowd, so by default, everyone supposedly liked her.

"Yep, we'll be there!" Phebe confirmed, with an equally fake smile. Phebe couldn't make her long, light-brown ringlets bounce the way Pelin's hair did, but she did manage to make her curls shimmy just a little.

"Cool beans." Pelin flashed her mouthful of big white teeth, showing off the results of the new *Nature's Way* tooth whitening paste that had recently hit the market. "Can't wait to catch up with you ladies!" The two pom captains disappeared into a cloud of their own perfumes.

Being on the pom squad was one way that middle-class girls like Joanna and Phebe, and their other closest friend Lisa, could make a name for themselves within the walls of Liberty High School. The team performed pom routines to all pep band songs, but since the routines were simple and nameless, they were just called "Boring #1," "Boring #2," or whichever number within the eight routines they represented. As much as Joanna liked being on Poms, she could take or leave the team captains. Pelin and Dana were snarky and gossipy, and Joanna simply didn't really like either of them.

Phebe wrapped her arms around her best friend for a hug. Then she rolled her eyes at what they had just witnessed and said, "Whatever. But speaking of schedule changes, I heard Aaron Mickels say that he now has Econ second hour..."

"Oooh," Joanna sang as Phebe darted into the room across the hall.

***

Joanna was classified as an average-looking girl, but she was pretty in her own right. At a slender five-foot-eight, she had dark blond hair and bright, blue-green eyes. Her one dimple on her left cheek only revealed itself when she smiled a certain way, as well as sometimes when she talked or laughed. Occasionally, a glow of health and beauty radiated from her, but that beauty was dulled by her position on a mid-level rung of the social ladder.

"We only have a few weeks before Hawaii," Pelin announced that afternoon, during the pom practice. "So we can't get sloppy." She may have thought she was being subtle when she glared at one of the juniors on the squad, but Joanna caught it.

It was a typical afternoon of pom practice: review of the Borings, then more preparation for the performances for the Spring Break band trip to Honolulu. And, of course, criticism from Pelin and Dana, whenever they felt someone wasn't pulling their share of the load. Joanna, Phebe, and Lisa were well-trained at 42nd Street Dance Studio in town, but there were times when others on the squad were called out for not being up to standard. Phebe claimed that the criticism from their captains was justified, and that the juniors needed to up their game a bit. But Joanna often felt the criticism was mean and could be more effective with a kinder delivery.

"I can see why Pelin's not your favorite person," Lisa said to Joanna and Phebe that afternoon, as the three girls walked to Joanna's family car in the high school parking lot after pom practice. Joanna pulled out her 42nd Street Dance Studio lanyard with the heavy ring of keys on it. Carrying around a lanyard with a bunch of keys was something all the cool kids did. The rich kids all had their own cars, but you were still somewhat cool if you at least had a car to drive once in a while. And if you swung around your long lanyard with keys ever-so-casually as you talked or walked to the car, you were definitely right up there with the rich kids. Having the lanyard and a car to use was enough "cool" for Joanna; she didn't need to swing them around, so she held the keys close.

"*Peelin' Potatoes* just bugs me," Joanna complained, mocking her peer's name.

Phebe bellowed out dramatically in a deep, theatrical voice, "*Peeeeeelinnnn potatoes!*" and Joanna immediately cupped her mittened hand over Phebe's mouth. She looked around to be sure no one else was within earshot, and all three girls burst into giggles.

The nickname for Pelin had come about years ago when Joanna first decided she didn't like the girl whose name rhymed with words that described all sorts of shady activities. She and Phebe made up a song, which the three girls now chanted quietly as they approached Joanna's car. *"She's a wheelin' dealin' boyfriend-stealin' don't-care-if-she-hurts-their-feelins... She's a girl with a dumb name! Potatoes are her game! She's peel-innnnn potatoes!"*

It was a silly, immature song, with no real tune, but it made the girls laugh when they had to deal with their unpleasant pom squad captain.

Joanna fumbled through her thick mittens to unlock the car, as the brisk January wind danced gently across her face. She was grateful that she could be open with her two best friends about her disdain for their peer, even though Phebe strived to be 'cool.' Phebe didn't like Pelin either, but at school, there was an image to maintain. Phebe placed more value on that image, and she expected Joanna to be cool with her. Joanna was cool within their own circle, and she had no desire to be any more than that. There were many things running rampant within the upper crust crowd that made Joanna uncomfortable, like alcohol and sex. Lisa didn't care about keeping up an image – she had bigger fish to fry with having a drunk mother, no father, and two older brothers that had already been in and out of jail. The fact that Lisa didn't care about an image made her cool, but again, only within their middle-class circle. The upper crust circle was a whole other story. Nonetheless, Lisa was a very safe friend to Joanna, especially when Joanna needed an ally in her value system.

"We just have a few more weeks until Hawaii," Lisa quoted the pom captains, once Phebe had been dropped off at home. "That's only a couple of games! And then we're done with Poms forever and we won't have to deal with Pelin anymore."

"Yep, *after tomorrow*," Joanna smiled, citing Mr. Charmin and appreciating the perspective. "Speaking of that, you can ride with us to the hockey game on Saturday if you want. Christopher and I are going early."

January, 1995

Hallo, Herr Journal! (That's "Mr. Journal," for those of you who don't speak German.) Welcome to my life! My name is Joanna Marie Conors, I am eighteen years old, and I live in Woodland Hills, Minnesota. My best friend Phebe gave me this book for Christmas, and she told me to name you "Herr Journal" because I like speaking German. Phebe doesn't keep a journal; she says she has nothing to write, and even if she did, she wouldn't bother. But she says I have a lot to write, and she knows I will bother.

These next few months are going to be exciting! My twin brother Christopher and I are going to Hawaii (!) on the band trip during Spring Break. He plays trumpet, and I am a dancer on the pom squad. Christopher has a girlfriend, Nicole, who plays clarinet. She's super nice; I really like her. I don't have a boyfriend, but I have a lot of friends. Phebe is my very best friend, and Lisa is our other best friend. We're all on Poms together, and we also dance together at 42nd Street Dance Studio. My other closest friend is Matthew, who is Christopher's best friend, but he's kind of my best bud too. My *Freundschafts* (friendships – another German word) are very important to me, and I worry about what will happen "after tomorrow" (as my English Lit teacher Mr. Charmin calls it) when we graduate.

Christopher, Matthew, and I all have part-time jobs at the Toy Store, which is a big retail chain in our town's shopping center. I need spending money for Hawaii, and Christopher and I are also going to Germany in June with our German class… I have to save, save, save!

Jodie, who is sixteen, is my only sister, and I have another brother, Nick, who is ten. My dad works at the bank, and my mom is a teacher. I want to be a teacher too – I'll be going away to college in the fall to the University of Wisconsin in Timberwood. I guess that's all you need to know about me for now! ☺

Chapter 2: The Toy Store

The Toy Store, a big international retail toy chain with a store in Woodland Hills, was where Joanna, her twin brother Christopher, and their close friend Matthew Carmichael all had part-time jobs. While Joanna didn't always feel popular or socially competent at school, at the Toy Store, she was quite proficient. At the Toy Store, Joanna mostly worked in the Customer Service Area, greeting shoppers as they came and went, assisting the cashiers when they had problems, helping customers with refunds or questions, and answering the phones. She knew her job, and she liked helping the shoppers.

During the holiday season, the Toy Store tripled its staff with temporary employees, but almost all of them were laid off after inventory in January. Only a few would remain on staff and become permanent, and now that the season was over, the handful of 'keepers' were officially welcomed as regular employees.

Luke Mason was one of the newly-welcomed keepers on the staff. He was a few years older than Joanna and Christopher, and nobody had paid any attention to him while he was lumped in with all the other seasonal hires. He was usually assigned to work on the salesfloor, putting out new merchandise and keeping the shelves stocked. Now that the dust had settled from the craziness of holiday shopping, Joanna was asked to train him in as a cashier.

"I thought all the seasonals were trained to cashier first and foremost?" Joanna wondered aloud to Deb on Saturday morning, when she clocked in for her shift. Deb was a supervisor in the Customer Service Area, with whom Joanna got along really well. Joanna hadn't met Luke yet, or at least she didn't think she had, but she knew he was seasonal, and all seasonal employees should have been trained as a cashier before anything else.

Deb, a woman in her mid-forties, shook her head in annoyance and replied, "He was, I'm sure, but..." She lowered her voice to a whisper. "He's terrible! He needs a refresher on... everything!"

Joanna smiled. She liked teaching people, and she certainly knew all the ins-and-outs of cashiering! She appreciated Deb's bluntness, to know what she was getting into that day.

A few minutes later, a short, somewhat-burly man with plain, clear-framed glasses sauntered coolly toward the Customer Service Area. His receding hairline seemed premature for someone who couldn't be too far into his twenties yet. He didn't say anything, but once Joanna saw him, she remembered him walking around the store during the holiday season. She recalled her first impression of him – an impression that was not impress*ive*. She thought quietly in her head, *This guy made it through the seasonal cuts?* What she remembered from seeing him around during the holiday season was that he usually appeared to be doing nothing.

Deb must have read the look on Joanna's face, and she whispered, "Yes, we're keeping him, I guess. He has daytime availability and is willing to do overnights when needed. So, train him well, because I may be stuck with him as a cashier during the week!" She cleared her throat once Luke was near her and declared, "Luke, this is Joanna. The two of you will be working together today. She's in charge, so make sure you listen to the things she teaches you."

Deb walked away, and Joanna said confidently, with her warm smile, "Alright, Luke, Christmas season at the Toy Store is when we are in survival mode. Everybody just does what they have to do to get through the day, and a lot of stuff slips through the cracks. Now that things have settled down and we have time to actually breathe, we need to solidify some of the basics of the different jobs here at the store."

Outside of the Toy Store, Joanna was never very outgoing, as she was far more comfortable observing others and staying in her place on the side. She followed the rules and did what she was supposed to do, and never called attention to herself. At the Toy Store, however, she was confident in her job, and the management looked to her to be a leader. Therefore, here, she was quite dynamic, which was intriguing to a newcomer like Luke.

"So," she went on as he nodded, and they walked over to Register 2. "This is how we will do things today. I will ring up the sales for a while, and you can watch. I will explain everything I'm doing, as if you are brand new and have never done this ever before. Later, we will switch places, and you will take over, but I will be right here in case anything weird comes up. Sound like a plan?"

Luke just looked at her. The silence felt long. There were no customers at the moment, so he said, "Who *are* you?" There was a hint of a smile in his eyes, behind those boring round glasses.

Joanna gave him a confused look. "I just told you. I'm Joanna, the person who is going to train you."

"No, *you* didn't tell me that. *Deb* told me that."

Joanna rolled her eyes. *Great,* she thought. *This guy is going to split hairs.*

"But who *are* you?" Luke repeated, and then he went on, "Are you, like, Wonder Woman at the Toy Store, or..."

A man and his son came up to the register then, and they set a Space Rangers action figure on the counter. Joanna turned to Luke and whispered, "I'm here to teach you how to do your job, so pay attention." Then she stepped into the register console and greeted the customers cheerfully. "How are you guys today?" She pressed a button on the register to start the transaction.

"It's my brother's birthday tomorrow!" the boy declared energetically. "This is his present, but don't tell him."

"Oooh!" Joanna responded. Her eyes were wide and dramatic, as she picked up the Space Ranger and scanned it with the scanner. "And you got the blue one! That's, like, the hardest one to find, you know."

"I know, we can't believe it!" the happy dad cried. "What's the deal with that, anyway? There are about twenty green and red ones out there, and only one blue one."

Joanna smiled. "That's how they create the demand," she told him. "They only send us one blue one for about every ten green or red ones, I think. Then no one can get a blue one... except for *you*, for your *brother*!" She looked at the little boy with her sparkling eyes, and he jumped up and down excitedly. She winked at him and said to the dad, "Your total is $9.56, sir."

The man paid with cash, Joanna counted out his change, and she handed him the receipt. When they left, Luke just looked at her again. "You must think I'm a real dumbass if you think I couldn't do that sale myself," he said.

Joanna thought for a minute before responding. She wasn't sure she liked this co-worker, as he seemed a bit... difficult. But something about him was interesting. After a moment, she said, "I'm sure you could have handled that sale yourself, but I was asked to re-teach you anyway."

"Why? Did the managers say I don't know what I'm doing?" he challenged her defensively.

Not wanting to offend this person she had just met, Joanna tried to remain tactful in her reply. "I think everyone who was seasonal gets to go through refresher training now."

"Well, I know how to cashier," he told her sharply. "I just hate it, so I acted like I didn't know what I was doing. And it worked! Every time they put me on a register, they'd get sick of me asking so many questions and they'd end up sending me back to the floor!"

This sounded like the most ridiculous thing ever to Joanna. "Why would you make yourself look stupid on purpose?" she asked him incredulously.

"Because I hate cashiering!" Luke repeated in exasperation. "I don't want to talk to people and be all *Oh you got the blue one! Wow! How lucky for your birthday!*"

Joanna just looked at him, and Luke started to laugh. She squinted her eyes disgustedly, and the bright blue-green color of them pierced him with contention through her dark lashes. "Why are you working in a toy store if you're so bitter?"

Luke held up his hand and rubbed his thumb against his fingertips, making a good point: The Toy Store paid a higher hourly wage than other area retailers.

"Well, you'd better learn to fake it, then," she informed him, her eyes still fiery and her voice turning cold. Joanna was protective of her Toy Store, and she didn't want antagonistic people working at it. And she didn't have patience for people who put money before good character. "Because now that the holiday season is over, hours are limited and you don't get to pick the position they give you for your shift. So, you need to be competent in all areas, including cashiering."

Luke made a face and mocked, "Ohhh-okay-ay." But he was smiling, and he promised Joanna he would shape up.

Another co-worker walked by then, and hollered out in a friendly tone, "JOANNA CONORS!" It was a slow day for cashiering, and the rest of the staff were busy reworking aisle layouts and setting up Valentine's Day displays. Mike Grenzesky, who was old enough to be in college but was only taking a class or two here and there, liked Joanna, and he found any excuse to talk to her during their shifts. He was nice, so she was always polite to him, even though she sometimes found his 'nice-ness' to be a tad bit annoying. Mike stopped at Register 2 and just stood there.

"Yessss, Mike?" Joanna asked him, half-impatiently and half with a tone of mystery. Mike often stopped by wherever she was in the store when they worked together, just to say hi and bellow out her name.

"You goin' to the hockey game tonight?"

Liberty High School's hockey games were a big deal in town, and they were usually sold out. There weren't too many teams close by to play, so games often took place out of town up in the Twin Cities. On this night, however, the game would be in town, and it was going to be an event.

"Of course!" Joanna replied enthusiastically. "I'll be pomming at it!" She reached out her arms and shook her fists from her wrists.

"Great! I'll watch for you!" Mike promised. "You're playing my alma mater, and we're gonna whip your butts."

"You went to Cannon Valley High School?" Joanna asked him curiously, referencing the neighboring town that Liberty would be playing that night. "I thought you lived here in Woodland Hills."

"I do," he told her. "But I grew up in Cannon Valley."

"Oh."

"See you tonight, Joanna. I'll be watching you." Mike walked away.

"He *soooo* wants you," Luke joked quietly.

"Shut up."

"So, you're a pom girl?"

"Yep! So, since you're so good at cashiering, even though you pretended not to be, do you think you're ready to do the next one yourself?"

"Nope."

Joanna sighed. She told him tiredly, "You know, Luke, the sooner you show me that you're competent at this, the sooner we can be done with this training." He was already wearing her out.

"I kinda like the training," he said.

Joanna again detected the twinkle in his eye, even from behind his boring glasses. "Great. Then show me that you've actually learned something so that I know my training was effective."

"What are you, a teacher?" he asked her with a half-laugh.

"I will be someday," she told him proudly. She stepped out from the register console and motioned for him to step in. "Now go!" A woman came up to them with a cart full of toys, and Luke started the transaction.

I had to train this weird seasonal guy at work today. He was so difficult! I don't know why he's working at a toy store since he seems to hate it, but it was kind of fun training him anyway. His name is Luke, and I liked it because I like teaching. He needs a lot of help with his people skills, though. Tonight is a hockey game in town. Mike G. from work says he's coming, and he's going to watch me perform. That's kind of cool – I love performing.

Chapter 3: The Lists

The arena was a full house that night, and since Cannon Valley was so close, many of the fans were there to support the visiting team. The drumming of Liberty's pep band echoed throughout the dome, and the pom girls lined up along the steps of two concrete aisles, ready to perform.

In between songs, the pom squad sat together and talked. Pelin was always good at stirring up gossip, and Phebe usually jumped right on it. The pom squad paid no regard to social order, which was fortunate for Joanna, Phebe, and Lisa. Extra-curriculars like Poms blended the worlds of the upper crusters and middle-class girls, and somehow, there, it was okay for the two groups to mix.

Phebe had been Joanna's best friend for*ever*, and their long history of friendship cemented their loyalty to each other. Although Joanna sometimes felt that Phebe's participation in gossip was not the best use of her energy, she appreciated the "in" she had to the lives of the elite, thanks to Phebe.

Grant McAllister, a classmate who played in the band, came over to the group to flirt with Dana, the other pom captain, for a few minutes. When he went back to his place with the drumline, one of the girls asked Dana, "What was that all about?"

"She's on his list," Pelin answered for her, slyly.

Dana just smiled and said, "Yeah, well, Pelin, you're on Troy Milbourne's list."

"So? So is Violet. And Joanna. Joanna's on Troy's list too!" Pelin announced.

Phebe had been watching this, but once they mentioned Joanna, they really had her interest. Phebe jumped in with, "Wait! What's this *list* you're talking about?"

"The list!" Pelin affirmed smugly, trying to sustain the mystery. Even though the pom squad was blind to social order, Pelin still liked to uphold her higher status whenever she could.

As Joanna watched this interaction, she decided that Pelin ought to lighten up on the make-up. Pelin was already beautiful enough with her olive skin and solid brown eyes. Most people envied her long, silky black hair, with its caramel streaks layered perfectly throughout her mop, thanks to the local upscale salon. She didn't really need the heavy eye-liner and sparkly shadow too. And she didn't *need* a whole pound of mascara weighing down those lashes on her seductive eyelids, either.

Dana, who somehow pulled off still looking feminine and trendy even with her short, wavy, brown, almost-boyish hair, leaned over to Phebe and Joanna and said quietly, "All the guys are making lists of who they want to sleep with in our class. Troy has Pelin and Violet on his."

"And Joanna!" Pelin called over from two seats away. "Troy has Joanna on his list too!" While the popular girls felt complimented to be on a guy's list, Pelin spoke as though she knew Joanna would be offended.

Not wanting to affirm Pelin's suspicion, Joanna remained expressionless, though her eyes widened slightly.

"Oooh, Jay! You made a list!" Phebe marveled with a cunning smile, using Joanna's peer-group nickname. Joanna detected that Phebe loved the idea of her best friend being on a popular guy's list, since they were only middle-class. This would make Phebe, by default, cool too. At least that was the assumption.

Joanna wasn't impressed, however. Her first thought was *That's disgusting!* But she knew enough to never react so prudishly to these girls, so she settled with a sweet smile and asked, "Who else has a list?" Dana had said "all the guys," but did that mean just all the popular guys? Or did that include the middle-class guys too? Band was another area that paid no regard to social order, so Joanna wondered if her brother and Matthew had lists as well.

"They *all* do!" Dana confirmed with a smirk. "Phebe, you're on Aaron Mickels' list. And also Dustin Rollick's and Shawn Mercer's, I think. They're all naming, like, the top five girls or whatever."

"Dustin Rollick??" Phebe couldn't help exclaiming in disbelief. She beamed, and Joanna knew exactly what she was thinking. Though Dustin Rollick was a slimebucket, he was popular and very good-looking. Aaron and Shawn were no big deal; they were middle-class. But Dustin Rollick was something!

"Jo-aaaa*nna*..." Pelin teased in a sing-songey voice. Joanna's reputation for being ultra-traditional, which many people appreciated and respected, was nothing but annoying to Pelin, so Pelin took this opportunity to make Joanna the oddball.

After a pause, Joanna maintained a fake smile and said, "I'm not sure this is anything to be proud of."

"Oh, take a chill pill," Pelin snapped. "It's just a dumb boy game. You don't have to get all prissy and offended."

Violet Flite, the band's only baton twirler, rushed over and slid next to Dana. Violet didn't perform during hockey games, but she still sat with the band since she was technically part of that group. "Okay, I got the 411," she said hurriedly. Her chin-length, light-brown, spiral-permed curls bounced around her face. "Troy's list is me, Pelin, Tammy – sophomore Tammy – which... okay, *whatever*, and.... Joanna, of course, and Kaley and Shana."

"That's six," Dana pointed out. "They're only supposed to name five."

"I know," Violet said. Her tone was full of drama, as usual. "He says since Kaley and Shana are twins, he'll do a threesome and count them as one."

Upon hearing this, Joanna rolled her eyes. "So does my brother have a *list*?" she asked Violet, since Violet seemed to be in charge of the headlines this time.

Violet rolled her eyes now, as if this was the most boring question ever. Or, at least, it had the most boring answer ever. "Yeah, *Nicole*. She's the only one. I think he has to say that, since she's sittin' right next to him."

"Or maybe because they've been going out for, like, the whole year," Dana interjected with a tone of annoyance.

Lisa, who was sitting nearby, said to herself, "I'd better not be on anyone's list."

Dana heard her, and snapped immediately, "You're not." Her tone was sharp.

"Dana! That was mean!" Joanna cut in, jumping to her friend's defense.

"Wha-at?" Dana asked, now sounding innocent.

"That was mean. *You're not!*" Joanna quoted her.

"Well, she *just said* she hoped she wasn't on a list, so I was reassuring her

After Tomorrow

that she has nothing to worry about!"

"Never mind." Lisa got up and walked away.

Joanna just looked at all the girls around her. Pelin, Dana, Violet... all sitting there, all proud, to be on a guy's list of who he wants to have sex with. Most of these girls – probably all of them, in fact – were already having sex with guys from school. There were many things that Joanna would miss about high school once she graduated, but she wouldn't miss these catty girls.

"Nathan Hooks has a list, Grant has a list, Aaron Mickels, Colvin, Troy..." Dana rattled off all the names.

Nathan Hooks. Joanna caught that name and tuned in again. Nathan Hooks, the very popular guy who had been in school with her for four years, still ignored her in their homeroom every day. Joanna was sure Nathan Hooks would never give someone in the middle-class group the time of day.

"Does Matthew Carmichael have a list?" Phebe asked devilishly, bringing her closest friends into the mix. This question ripped Joanna's thoughts away from Nathan, as she now listened intently for the answer about Matthew. Joanna had a unique connection with her brother's best friend that seemed to grow stronger each year. Matthew was a good-looking guy, very kind and funny, but since he didn't draw a lot of attention to himself, people often missed out on his subtle sense of humor. His friendship with Joanna was rather special, and lately Joanna noticed herself feeling protective of it.

"Pfff!" Dana scoffed. "Matthew! He's such a tease." She scrunched up her face and mocked what apparently was Matthew's response to the question of having a list: "*I do have a list, but I would never dream of revealing who is on it. I'd have girls pounding down my doors every weekend if my list was made public!*" Suddenly Dana's short, wavy boy-hair didn't make her look quite so cute anymore, and Joanna silently giggled. That was such a 'Matthew' thing to say! Pelin muttered something about Matthew being a pastor's son, so of course he wouldn't admit to such a list, and again Joanna smiled. Matthew always managed to stay 'cool,' even with his traditional values.

Liberty High School's hockey team scored a goal then. The crowd cheered, and it was time for another Boring. The pom girls quickly jumped into their places on the steps of the aisles and waited for Pelin or Dana to announce which number.

"SIX!" Pelin called out, and all the girls held their poms up, ready for the music to start.

After Boring #6 was done, Joanna was startled to find Mike Grenzesky and Luke Mason from the Toy Store, now sitting in the end seats next to the aisle where she was standing. "Oh!" she exclaimed in surprise, when she turned around to set down her poms. "Where did you guys come from?!"

"We've been here all night, Conors, what do ya mean?" Mike teased her. He was wearing a red Cannon Valley Cannons sweatshirt and a red and white CVC ski hat.

"You have not," she disputed, and Luke laughed.

"FOUR!" Pelin called out, and the drums started up for another song.

"Well, go back to your seats!" Joanna said hurriedly as she grabbed her poms again. She jumped into position, ready for Boring #4.

"Nah, we can watch ya from right here," Mike smiled.

Joanna faced the ice rink now. She stood straight in position for the first count, but her heart was racing with nerves. These two guys from her work were now sitting right at eye level of her butt, with her short pom skirt and her long, skinny legs. She was *not* okay with this!

As the song started up, she focused on the rink below and made sure she wacked her arms more dramatically than she needed to, so that her poms might hit either Mike or Luke in the face. She hoped the guys would take the hint that these were not appropriate seats!

They did not take the hint, however, and the rest of the night was terribly uncomfortable. Joanna didn't want to be rude to them, but she was also annoyed that they were sitting *right there* and probably staring at her butt as she performed. There were other empty seats near these aisles; they didn't have to sit *right there*!

"Nice show, Conors," Mike winked at her when the game was over. He and Luke stood up as Joanna stuffed her poms into her giant pom bag. Joanna just forced a smile and skipped down the aisle steps to join up with Phebe and Lisa.

***

On Sunday night, Joanna tapped on Christopher's bedroom door as he was finishing up his homework at his desk. "Hi Big Brother," she said as she came into the room. Even though she was the first-born twin, she always referred to Christopher as *Big Brother*.

"Yo-Jo."

"Do we have to do all of page two for the Beowulf review sheet, or just the short answer part?"

"All of it. But the last part is just the connections questions, so it's not really that much."

"Oh. Okay."

Joanna lingered for a moment, hoping her brother's twinship radar would detect that she had something on her mind besides their English Literature assignment.

It did. He looked up at her. "What else? I didn't do my pre-calc yet, so I don't know anything about that assignment."

Joanna hesitated, and then she said carefully, "So... What's with the lists?"

"The lists? What lists?" he asked, probably wondering which assignment she was referring to.

"The *lists*," she repeated, as if that clarified everything. "Evidently you *guys* all have *lists* of which girls you want to sleep with..."

"Whaaat...?" he said slowly, as if he had no idea what she was talking about. But Joanna just looked at her brother and gave him *the look* – the look that reminded him who he was talking to; the look that told him it was no use trying to fake anything. "Oh," he finally conceded. "*That* list."

"Uh-huh. What is *that* all about?"

Christopher just shook his head, as if this was not even worth discussing. "It's just dumb guy-talk, Jo-Jo. It's all in fun."

"It's disgusting," she said, not amused. With her brother, she wasn't afraid to maintain her value system. Especially since she wanted to make sure *he* was maintaining their value system.

"Joanna, I don't think you need to bug out on this," he said gently.

Christopher was a good guy, and he valued his relationship with his sister. He understood that it was just her personality to take these things more seriously than she probably should, but even so, he wished she'd just relax sometimes! "First of all, you gals aren't even supposed to know about that. That's just guy-talk that girls don't understand, and girls end up taking it out of context. And second of all, since you do know about it, you should also understand that that's just part of being a guy. The guys were just joking around to say who they think is hot. You can't blame us for being guys!"

Joanna wasn't convinced. "I heard the list was who you want to *sleep* with."

"Well, yeah!" he affirmed with a laugh. "That's always the ultimate goal for a guy, isn't it?"

"What are you? Cavemen?" Joanna cried. "That's *so* disrespectful to all of us!"

"Would you chill, girl?" Christopher said, but still with his gentle tone. Even when Joanna got fired up, Christopher was always able to maintain his calm demeanor. "Don't worry about Matthew. He had to pick someone, so he just jokingly said *you* to get Dana off his back. Don't worry –"

"What?!" Joanna cried, this time shocked. "What do you mean, *He had to pick someone*? Matthew had *me* on his list?"

"Well, yeah! I thought that's what you were buggin' out about!"

"Dana said Matthew didn't have a list! She said he just flaked it off with a joke about not being able to reveal any names!"

Christopher rolled his eyes and leaned forward. "Jo-Jo, okay, first of all, *you* were on, like, *every* guy's list last night. I mean, seriously. I wanted to puke because you're my sister and I'm listening to all these jokers saying ...things... about you, and that you're so hot and all that, okay? And then they're razzin' me about you being my sister and yada-yada-yada. Whatever. And Dana doesn't like you because you're way cooler than she is – "

"I am not way cooler than Dana!" Joanna objected. "She's in the Troy Milbourne/Pelin Yilmaz group!"

"Yeah, so what?!" Christopher refuted. "The real men around the school all know you're super cool. At least, if they want a girl with any depth. Dana and Violet and Pelin and all those girls are all skanks."

Joanna knew she was 'quality,' but right now, in high school, quality wasn't popular. She was glad to know, though, that her brother and her real friends valued quality over popularity.

"And anyways," Christopher went on, "you're a better pommer than Dana is, and she knows it, and you know Dana, she's... she's *Dana*. And she kept demanding to know who was on everyone's list."

"I thought Violet was the one asking about the lists," Joanna interrupted again. Christopher was not answering all of her questions fast enough!

Christopher just shook his head. Sometimes he could not keep up with the intensity of his sister's emotions. "You know, all us guys were just sittin' there, jokin' around with each other, being guys, and those two busy-bodies jumped in and started badgering us about something that was none of their business. Those two are so annoying! You girls gotta know when you're supposed to just mind your own business!"

"Lisa and I were minding our own business."

"Fine. Whatever. So anyways, Dana and Violet and whoever were demanding to know who was on whose lists, and they were badgering Matthew. And yeah, he threw out some dumb response about all the chicks flocking to him if he were to reveal anything, so... whatever. But then Violet kept buggin' him to name *someone*, so he just jokingly said, *Okay, evidently I should say Joanna because she's on everyone else's list!* Or something like that."

Joanna waited a moment while she processed what she had just heard. This all made sense, sort of, though she wasn't sure how she felt about any of it. Finally, she shrugged and said, "Well, all those guys are pigs."

"Well, Matthew wasn't being a pig," Christopher said, defending his best friend.

"Well, I *know* Matthew isn't a pig. But all those other scrubs with lists are pigs. And did you see that Mike Grenzesky and that Luke-guy from work came to the game?"

"I thought I saw them over there!" Christopher exclaimed, clearly glad to have the subject changed. He sat up straighter. "They were right by you, right?"

"Yeah... That was weird. Is that weird?"

"I don't know."

"They were right at eye-level with my butt. I think that's weird."

"*They* probably like you too," Christopher suggested.

"Hmmm," she said softly. But then she went back to the lists. "Well, if the guys from school start talking about their *lists* again, tell them to take me off of them."

"Yes, ma'am."

So... Herr Journal... evidently part of being a guy at this age is making a "list" of girls you want to sleep with. And evidently, I am on a few of these lists. Even Matthew's! I don't even know what to think about that. I asked Christopher about it, and he blew it off as a dumb high-school boy thing. So, whatever, I guess.

On a different note, Mike G. from work came to our hockey game last night, and that seasonal guy Luke came with him. They sat right by me all night... It was pretty uncomfortable. Why are guys so weird??!

Chapter 4: Alone at Lunch

On Monday at school, the usual mixed-company group sat together during lunch.

"I can't believe you were on the lists of the guys in *that* group!" marveled Nicole Sheldon, Christopher's girlfriend. "That's amazing. Those guys usually don't cross over to us peasants."

"Well, Pelin and Violet and those girls are all used up, so the guys are bound to start trollin' elsewhere eventually!" Joanna joked. After giving it a day for the dust of her thoughts to settle on this, she had relaxed about it.

While Phebe and the others continued analyzing the list situation before their guy friends joined them, Joanna looked up and noticed Laura Vigent, a girl that was in her pre-calc class. Laura was standing alone, holding her lunch tray, in the middle of the cafeteria. She looked completely lost.

Joanna nudged Lisa and said quietly, "Why is Laura Vigent just standing there?" Laura was definitely not in the popular crowd; she didn't even make it to the middle-class group. She was a simple girl, who most people paid no attention to. But today, after becoming bored with the discussion of lists, Joanna noticed her.

Lisa looked over in Laura's direction and shrugged. "I don't know. She was in here the other day, too, eating by herself. She's not normally in this lunch hour, is she?"

Joanna shook her head. "I don't think so." They watched as Laura finally carried her tray over to the empty end of a table, and sat down, alone.

The discussion of lists was done, but Joanna's table was still buzzing with unimportant chatter. Phebe was telling a story about her economics class: "...And then Aaron was like, *I think it was the Judicial Branch...*" Sometimes Phebe's stories got long.

Joanna tuned Phebe out and watched Laura. "She's sitting all by herself!" she said worriedly to Lisa.

"I know," Lisa said. "She sat there the other day, too, by herself." The girls waited another minute to see if anyone else would join her, but by then everyone had their seats for the lunch period.

Joanna stood up and walked over to Laura. She didn't know Laura at all, other than that Laura sat near her in her pre-calc class this year. Laura was quiet but seemed smart. Probably on a normal day, Joanna wouldn't have even noticed – or bothered with – someone sitting alone in the cafeteria, but on this day, her own circle had lost her interest, so Joanna decided to go over there.

"Hi Laura," Joanna said kindly, sitting across from her on the bench.

Laura looked up from her taco salad and said, "Oh, hi."

"Are you always in this lunch?" Joanna asked her.

"No, my schedule just changed. I had to drop my computer class," Laura explained. "So that changed my lunch hour."

"Well, would you like to sit with us?" Joanna offered. If there was one thing Mr. and Mrs. Conors had drilled into their children's heads ever since they were born, it was to *be kind*. Always, always, always put yourself in the other person's shoes and *be kind*. Lisa was already so good at being kind, and Joanna wanted to be like that too. So even though it might be awkward to have a newcomer at their lunch table, Joanna would not have been able to watch this girl sit by herself every day for the rest of the school year.

Laura's whole face relaxed, and she smiled. "Are you sure? I don't want to be a third wheel. Or a... I don't know... eighth wheel... extra wheel... or whatever..."

Joanna grinned and stood up. "We've got plenty of room for extra wheels," she said, leading the way back to her table. Laura sat down at the end but still kept to herself. While the others continued in their normal lunch conversations, Joanna was glad Laura wasn't sitting all alone.

There's this girl in my class named Pelin, Herr Journal.
What a dumb name. PEE-linn. Like peelin' potatoes, you
know? Anyways, she and this other chick named Dana are
the pom captains, so they boss us all around. And since
they're like the two most popular girls at Liberty, everyone is
supposed to like them. Phebe always wants us to fake liking
them, but that's a lot of work. I can't stand them!

I'm working on my *Freundschafts* for the rest of this year,
Herr Journal. (Yes, I just 'pluraled' the German word for
'friendship,' as if it were English. And now I 'verbed' the
word 'plural'... That's what I love about having a journal! I
can write however I want!)

Anyway!! I'm working on my *Freundschafts*. Today I
reached out to Laura Vigent, so she wouldn't have to sit alone
at lunch. We need more kind people at school, and fewer
nasty ones like Pelin and Dana and all those 'popular' girls.

Chapter 5: A Ride Home

On Tuesday night at the Toy Store, Mike Grenzesky was there when Joanna arrived for her evening shift. When she walked by, he bellowed cheerfully, "JOANNA CONORS!" from the inflatable snow tubes reset he was working on in the front seasonal section of the store.

"Hello, Mike," she said politely. *Hello* was a greeting she used formally for acquaintances. She reserved *Hi* or *Hey,* or even *Yo,* for people she considered friends. The people with whom she maintained valuable *Freundschafts* got the greetings to reflect that.

"Liberty Belle," Mike mumbled facetiously with a smile that was half-smirk, and half—in Joanna's opinion—dumb.

Joanna rolled her eyes playfully and continued on her way to the breakroom. The pom girls were known as Liberty High School's "Liberty Belles," a name that probably should be reconsidered, given society's trend to support political correctness.

At the end of the night, Mike overheard Joanna asking their manager, Ken Douglas, what time he thought they'd be done working. "I have to call my dad for a ride home," she told him. "So, I was wondering if we'll be out of here on time... The store looks kind of messy." Though Joanna appreciated that her parents had purchased an extra car for the family for her and her brother to use, it seemed like Christopher always got first dibs on it. Or, at least, it seemed like his social engagements were taking priority more and more often lately.

Ken nodded. Having recently just finished his New Manager Training cycle, he would now work permanently in the Woodland Hills Toy Store. He was a fun manager, and the employees were happy that he would get to stay. "I think we'll be out of here by ten," Ken told her.

"Okay, I'll go call him and let him know to shoot for ten o'clock."

"Wait, Joanna," Mike went up to her. "I can give you a ride home."

Joanna just looked at her co-worker. Mike was nice, and he was always friendly with her. She suspected he kind of liked her. She did not like him *like that*, but a ride home would probably be okay. It would certainly save her parents a trip out to the shopping center late at night, which they would appreciate.

"Are you sure?" she asked him. "It's okay – My dad had planned on coming out here."

"No, no, I'd be happy to! It's no problem at all," Mike assured her with a big smile.

Joanna hesitated, but then said, "Okay, Mike. Thank you."

***

"So, what are your plans after graduation?" Mike asked Joanna politely, as they drove away from the shopping area and onto the main road leading out of town. Although she and Mike often worked overlapping shifts, they really didn't know each other very well.

"I'm going to UW-Timberwood," she told him, as she watched the lights from the shopping center fade in the side rearview mirror. "I'll be living in the dorms and have a roommate."

"Oh no!" Mike teased her. "You're crossing the border?! You're not going to become a Packers fan, are you?"

The rivalry between Minnesota Vikings fans and Green Bay Packers fans was serious business, but Joanna just shrugged playfully. "I guess you never know! But I doubt it, since I don't care about football in the first place."

"You won't be able to show your face again at the Store if you come back wearing green and gold," he cautioned her.

Joanna understood that Mike was only joking around with her, though his warning had some merit to it. Vikings fans did not sit well with a Packer-backer in their midst. "I am going to Wisconsin to get an *education*," she clarified. "Not to support the Packers. I'm going to be a teacher!"

"Aww, you'll make a great teacher!" he said encouragingly. "I can totally see you as a teacher. Let me guess: Kindergarten."

"Ha! Maybe," Joanna replied. "My mom is a kindergarten teacher, and she loves it. If I had my choice, though, I think I'd go a little older. Maybe second or third grade." Joanna was very friendly, and she loved talking about her dream of becoming a teacher. She watched the road carefully, though, knowing Mike would need her navigation to get to her house. "You'll want to turn at that light up there, by the gas station," she told him then, as they approached an intersection. "And then just after the railroad tracks, you'll take a left onto a street where there's only a left – you can't go right."

"Okay," Mike nodded. "So, you're going to leave us in the fall?"

"Yep!" she answered firmly. "I've got students out there waiting for me! I can't stay around here forever!"

"Hmmm." Mike hit the blinker and turned at the stoplight by the gas station.

"Ken said that I can probably still stay on payroll at the Toy Store, and just come home and work one weekend a month or something, and during our breaks, like Thanksgiving and Christmas."

"Oh, that would be nice." Then, as they drove down the long country road, Mike said, "You know, I was thinking that I should take you out on a real date sometime."

Joanna's eyes widened in the dark, and she had to think quickly. She wasn't prepared for this! She wasn't sure she wanted to go on an official "date" with Mike Grenzesky!

"Oh?" she responded, to buy herself some time. She hoped her tone sounded neutral.

"Yeah. I noticed you and I both don't work Thursday night, so I could take you out to dinner and then we could go up to Afton and go skiing."

Skiing! Joanna had never been skiing, and this whole proposal sounded quite elaborate for a first date. Especially on a school night!

"Oh, shoot, that sounds fun, Mike!" she lied, while still trying to sound cheerful. "I have dance on Thursday nights, though. So that wouldn't work."

"Dance?"

"Yes, um... Yes, I dance on Thursday nights." That part was true.

"Oh. Where at? At that 42nd Street place?"

The 42nd Street Dance Studio was the only place in town that offered lessons for people interested in dance, and Joanna had been taking classes there for years with Phebe and Lisa. Her Thursday night instruction this year was truly for leisure, while others at the studio were preparing for their first regional competition in the summer. "Yes," Joanna confirmed, suddenly not wanting to share any more details about her personal life.

They passed the railroad tracks, and Joanna pointed to a hidden turn for Cambridge Court, the secluded, wooded street that she lived on. "It's wayyyy down there," she told him, hoping that Mike wouldn't pursue the idea of a date now that she had changed the subject.

He stopped the car at the end of the long driveway. "I can walk you to the door," he offered, pressing the release to his seat belt.

"Oh, that's okay, Mike," Joanna told him hurriedly, as she unfastened her own seat belt. "I can see my dad in the window – he'll make sure I get to the door." She smiled and added, "Thank you for the ride home."

"You're welcome, Joanna," he said as he refastened his seat belt.

I worked tonight, and Mike G. gave me a ride home. It was kind of weird... I don't know him that well, and I've only really talked to him at work, about work things. But he's nice. I think he might like me, maybe. He asked me out for a real date, to go skiing. I can't because I have dance... thank goodness... because I don't think I like him *like that*. He seems like the kind of guy that could be *too* nice, where it might be kind of gross. Or not cool. Or whatever. But at any rate, it was <u>nice</u> of him to bring me home.

Chapter 6: Pie Night

On Saturday, both Joanna and Christopher worked a day shift at the Toy Store. At four o'clock, when they were supposed to be done, Ken asked them if they'd like some extra hours and stay until close, which was nine o'clock. Joanna definitely wanted the extra hours, but Christopher had a date with Nicole and had to leave.

"Conors, you're here all night?" one of the storeroom guys asked, when he saw Joanna still up in the Customer Service Area later. Joanna got along well with the storeroom guys.

"Yep, extra hours," she answered.

"We're going to Dream Belle's after work tonight," he told her. "It's Pie Night. You should come!"

Pie Night at Dream Belle's, the local ice cream parlor, sounded fun, but Christopher had taken the car when he left at four o'clock. Joanna had planned to have one of her parents pick her up later when she was done working. "Hmmm," she said thoughtfully. She wished Matthew was working that night; he would have been a comfortable ride home. "Who else is going?" Maybe Deb or her friend Jill or someone would be willing to give her a lift. Going out to Dream Belle's after work could get late, and she felt silly having to involve her parents in a social event.

Just then, Mike Grenzesky walked up to the Customer Service Area and said, "I can give you a ride home later, Joanna, if you don't have a car here tonight."

Joanna thought for a moment. Mike wasn't really her first choice for a ride home, but it wouldn't be terrible. And Dream Belle's was only about five minutes away from her home, so the ride would be short.

***

"So, the rule is, you *have* to order pie," one of the storeroom guys instructed everyone playfully, when the group from the Toy Store got to the ice cream parlor. "Because it's Pie Night."

"French silk!" someone announced.

"Apple Spice!" another announced.

One of the salesfloor supervisors was there too, and she announced that she would be having Lemon Meringue.

Mike leaned close to Joanna and whispered, "What would you like, Joanna? It's my treat."

"Oh, Mike, that's not necessary," Joanna told him sweetly. "You're already giving me a ride home, and you gave me a ride the other night... Let me pay for yours." She wanted to keep this as non-date-like as possible.

"No, no," he said immediately. "I feel bad, I kind of chickened out the other night... I've got you covered. What kind do you want?"

Joanna's instincts kicked in, and her heart rate sped up. *Chickened out? What does he mean, he 'chickened out'?* she wondered, though she had a pretty good idea.

"And for you, miss?" the waitress looked down at Joanna, with a pen and notepad in hand. Joanna recognized her as the grown daughter of one of her father's co-workers at the bank. Small town Woodland Hills...

Joanna slunk down in her chair a bit, hoping the waitress wouldn't think she and Mike were a couple. "Oh... Um... I'll have banana cream, please," she stammered, looking blankly at the menu. As distracted as she now was, she still knew she would want banana cream pie. Banana cream was her favorite.

"I'm sorry, we're out of banana cream tonight," the waitress told her.

Joanna looked up at her, confused. "You're out..."

"Awww, it's okay," Mike said in a patronizing tone. He leaned closer to Joanna and reached for the menu. He had his other arm along the back of her chair. "How about French Silk?" he suggested, as if he were her special guardian.

I hate this! Joanna screamed silently inside her head. *Mike is being wayyyy too... gentlemanly! And they are out of banana cream pie!* She really had her heart set on her favorite pie at Dream Belle's.

"Hmmm? What do you think?" Mike pressed sweetly. "French Silk?"

"Yeah, sure, whatever," Joanna muttered, sitting stiff as a board. She set down the menu and stared straight ahead. She really wished she was home right now.

"And you can put hers on my ticket," Mike told the waitress confidently. "I'll have Rocky Road." He leaned back with a smile and let out an arrogant breath.

"Oh, no, Mike," Joanna jumped in. "I got it. It's fine."

"No! It's fine, Joanna."

Going out with her work friends was usually fun, but Joanna found it hard to stay with the banter that night. She was preoccupied with Mike's comment, and nervous now about riding home with him. Would he try to kiss her? What did he mean that he 'chickened out'? She desperately wished that one of her other work friends – Liz or Jill or Deb – someone she was more comfortable with – was there! She was pretty comfortable with the other storeroom guys, but they were kind of in their own little world that night, and she didn't know how she'd be able to talk to them alone – away from Mike – to hitch a ride at this point.

Mike insisted on paying for Joanna's pie when the waitress brought the tickets out, and this time, she didn't argue. The three-dollar slice of which she only ate the whipped cream wasn't worth the battle.

"Well, you ready?" Mike asked her when everyone stood up to leave.

"Sure," Joanna nodded, zipping up her jacket and trying to appear casual as she pulled on her mittens.

When they got into his car, he turned the heat on full blast. Joanna asked him if he remembered how to get to her house, and he said yes. Out of the corner of her eye, Joanna noticed Mike put his hand up to his mouth, breathe into it, and then smell. She wondered if he was checking his breath.

He pulled onto the long, wooded street, braking just before the end of the Conors' driveway. "I'll just park right here," he said casually, as he reached for the gear shifter. The car veered slowly onto the chunky snow along the edge of the street, to the side of what was plowed.

Joanna disabled her seat belt and said bluntly, "You don't have to park, Mike. This is fine." She grabbed her purse and opened the door to let herself out. "Thank you for the pie and the ride." She slammed the door shut and trotted quickly up her driveway, carefully stepping along the slick pavement.

Tonight was really awkward. A bunch of us from the Toy Store went to Dream Belle's after work, and Mike Grenzesky gave me a ride. He paid for my pie, even though I didn't want him to, and I think he hoped to kiss me before he dropped me off. I need to be clear, Herr Journal: I DO NOT LIKE HIM LIKE THAT. To be honest, he sort of gives me the creeps. I am not having him give me a ride home anymore.

Chapter 7: Hockey Game Gossip

The bell on *Big Ben* echoed through the main hall, signaling the start of a new week. Mondays always seemed to come too quickly, and this morning brought with it frazzled teachers and late students from an overnight dumping of snow.

"I imagine our missing friends are out battling the icy roads right now," Mr. Charmin stated, looking around the room. His stern, monotone voice seemed louder on this morning. "I don't know why they didn't call it a snow day. It's not worth the risk of all you teen drivers out there skidding through town just to get to school on time."

The desk behind Joanna was empty. Mr. Charmin wrapped up his Homeroom duties and started their English Literature discussion, and then, Nathan Hooks entered the room. After handing the teacher his late pass, Nathan and his trail of Calvin Klein *Obsession for Men* sauntered coolly to his seat in the back of room. Joanna glanced up as he passed her, just in time to catch what seemed to be a split-second of eye contact, and an almost-smile on his face.

***

"Like, a *smile*-smile?" Phebe clarified excitedly as she, Joanna, and Lisa raced to the cafeteria for lunch later. "Like, not to be confused with just a plain old generic, *I just got away with being late* smile?"

"Yes! I'm sure of it," Joanna reported. "Eye contact and everything! Seriously, he has *never* looked at me during that class before! I was pretty sure he didn't know who sits in front of him!"

The girls got in line for the Monday special: a "hamburger" with a cold piece of cheese slapped on it, and a heap of fat potato fries flavored with steak seasoning.

"Well, you look really pretty today," Lisa complimented her, gently fingering a section of Joanna's long, dark-blond hair from behind her shoulder. "I like this tiny braid-twist thing you've got goin' on."

"You like this?" Joanna confirmed with a smile, turning her head to the side. She herself was quite pleased with how her first attempt at the 'do had turned out that morning, glad that her pink wool pom-pom hat hadn't messed it up on the way to school.

Knowing how much Joanna loves pickles, the head lunch lady, Mrs. Toley, piled a mountain of dill burger chips onto Joanna's tray and slid it out to her. The pale green juice seeped into the nearby fries, slightly soaking them. "Thank you, Mrs. Toley!" Joanna called out cheerfully. After learning about 'positive reinforcement' in last semester's Psychology class, she hoped to secure herself extra pickles every Monday.

"You're welcome, dear," Mrs. Toley responded with a nod, and, knowing Joanna would want Ranch dressing for her potato fries, she added, "The Ranch is over by the salad table."

"Yes, I like your hair today," Lisa affirmed, taking her own tray. "And I'll bet Mr. GQ liked it too!"

"Okay, so yeah, I got the smile," Joanna went on, returning to the original matter at hand. "But then! I didn't tell you this yet! When he sat down, he leaned forward and whispered, *What'd I miss?!*"

Phebe's eyes widened as she took her tray. "You're kidding, Jay! Okay, he *soooo* knows who you are! This was the perfect opportunity to start talking to you! He's probably been waiting all month for this!"

"Yeah, it took a blizzard and a late pass for Mr. Gorgeous to finally have the balls to talk to me. Wow."

✳✳✳

The following Saturday night was another hockey game, and this one was dragging on. "Aw man!" Phebe screeched in frustration as the North St. Paul Polars blocked yet another shot. "How did that not get in there?" It seemed that neither team could score.

"FIVE!" Pelin called out to the girls on the squad. The pom girls immediately shot into starting position, and then performed their Boring #5 routine as the pep band played *Proud Mary*. When the song was over, Joanna, Phebe, Lisa, and the two other girls in their aisle sat down in their cluster of seats near the band. Pelin and Dana soon joined them.

"At what point do they just call it a night?" Lisa wondered, as she looked at her watch.

"Oooh, there's Trina Nermals," Pelin said quietly, ignoring Lisa's question and leaning close to Joanna. One of the Junior girls from school walked by, carrying a tray of nachos and cheese.

Coming from gossips like Pelin and Dana, a statement like that could lead to anything. Joanna didn't really know Trina, but figured Pelin would elaborate if given the opportunity. So, playing innocent, Joanna offered as a response, "Those nachos look good!"

The class clown, Udo Meikler, who did not play in the band but loved hanging out with the girls and was usually pretty entertaining, came down to sit by this group now, just as Pelin was about to spill her gossip. Udo's real name was Will Meikler, but his German name during German class was Udo. When he got his German name freshman year, the name stuck, and he'd been known as "Udo" ever since.

"Trina Nermals had sex with Mark Hawkins last week after the hockey game," Pelin went on with a devilish gleam in her eye. "Mark said they did it in the back of the instrument storage room at school after everyone went back there to return their stuff."

Udo jumped right in to clarify all the parts to this story. "Mark Hawkins is a hockey player, Yilmaz," he pointed out. "Why would he be back at school after the game, in the instrument storage room? Trina Nermals isn't even in band either!"

Dana slapped Pelin on the leg. "You're gettin' your stories mixed up!" she scolded her friend. "Trina and Mark did it in the boys' locker room last week, because Mark's dad is the custodian and Mark got the keys. Troy Milbourne is the one who did it in the instrument storage room, with Jenna Stoker."

"Okay," Pelin took a quick breath and looked up at the bright arena lights to gather her thoughts. "So, Trina, Jenna, Stacy..." Then she lowered her voice and said, "*Violet* but nobody's supposed to know about that..."

"Violet!" Udo exclaimed in a loud, exasperated whisper. "No kidding, Yilmaz! Dish the dirt!" He clapped his hands together and leaned forward.

"Are these all the girls who have had sex?" Phebe asked, just waiting for more gossip. Phebe was good at picking up on social cues, even if she wasn't directly part of the activity. Joanna was also good at following the social cues, but while Phebe wasn't afraid to show her interest, Joanna kept quiet and just observed.

"Yeah, all the girls who aren't virgins," Dana told her hurriedly. They continued listing names of girls in their class.

"I don't remember what the story was with Violet," Pelin said. "I just remember hearing that she did it at a party with someone over Winter Break." Then she turned to Dana. "What about Nicole?"

Dana looked at Joanna. "Have your brother and Nicole done it yet?"

"Ooh, yeah, JC!" Udo exclaimed dramatically. "What's the scoop with Christopher and Nicole? They've been going out for a long time!"

Joanna was done with this conversation now. She couldn't believe how flippant her peers were being about sexual activity among high school students. "Are these things really anyone's business?" she asked.

"Oh, Joanna, don't worry," Dana told her in a patronizing tone. "Your day will come."

"*My* day will come?" Joanna repeated, pretending to be confused. She knew exactly what Dana meant, but she played dumb since Dana's intention was to be mean.

Luckily, saving face for Joanna, Udo joked, "Oh, Joanna's had her day, haven't you, JC?" He winked at her. "I heard you and Matthew Carmichael were gettin' it on in Mr. Determan's office."

Joanna burst into giggles and slapped her classmate on the arm. "Udo, shut up!" She relaxed now, and leaned back in her seat and put her foot up on the seat in front of her. She could handle Udo and his banter, knowing he wasn't out to hurt people. It was Pelin and Dana she didn't like.

"Yeah! I heard all about it!" Udo went on playfully. "You and the Mattster..." Udo pumped his hips back and forth in his seat.

Joanna giggled again and rolled her eyes. "You're such a dork," she joked with him, completely ignoring all the other ears that were lingering nearby. She remembered how just before Winter Break, she and Matthew had been brought to the office of the school guidance counselor, Mr. Determan, to go over some paperwork for some college credits they would be earning during spring semester. A big rumor started up that they were in trouble, but it was all just dumb high school repartee. Joanna knew that Udo knew the real story about that, so she got a kick out of his joke. She didn't care what any of the other gossips thought.

"Ooh, JC, put your leg down, you're turning me on!" Udo advised her briskly, and Joanna immediately dropped her leg. She didn't mind this kind of banter. Udo was always talking to everyone, joking with them, and being playful. He wasn't piggish – or mean – like other guys who might make such references.

I just don't like Pelin, Herr Journal. And I'm not impressed by Dana, either, to be perfectly honest. Tonight at the hockey game they were talking about all the girls in our class who are not virgins. How do they know these things?? And why are we talking about it? It's just sad to me that people our age treat sex so casually. And if someone asks you whether you're still a virgin, what's the right answer? If you say yes, then you're not cool, you're a loner, a prude, you're uptight, you're a goody-goody... But if you say no, then WHOA! You're a slut, you're a tramp, but you're also cool, I guess, by whatever the standard of 'cool' is by those measuring it.

And then there was a comment about me and Matthew... ☺

Chapter 8: Off to Hawaii

Spring Break this year was sure to be an adventure. Liberty High School's marching band and pom squad would be going to Hawaii for ten days in March, to perform at various functions and see the sites in Honolulu. This first big trip without their parents for Joanna and Christopher was one the twins couldn't wait for. Many of their friends were going, and it was an opportunity to get to know their other peers in a different context. Nobody on the pom squad had been to Hawaii before, but Pelin told everyone that there would be male strip clubs, and the girls would all be able to get into them if they wanted.

"I heard that they have these little underground places that can make fake IDs," she told her teammates during their last pom practice before the trip. She pulled open a snack-size bag of Doritos and started crunching on the chips.

"I'm in!" Dana announced happily. The popular girls were always rule-breakers, which made Joanna uncomfortable.

Phebe turned to Joanna and Lisa and whispered, "If we can get fakes, I'm in too!"

Joanna got a lump in her stomach during this conversation, but she didn't say anything. She was a rule follower, and the idea of going to a strip club with a fake ID scared her. If she got caught and her parents found out, she would die!

And besides, a strip club sounded so... *icky*.

As they drove home together after pom practice that day, Joanna confided her concerns to Lisa. "What do you think about this strip club idea?" she asked her. Lisa was level-headed and very gentle when responding to people, and Joanna never felt judged by her.

Lisa shrugged as she adjusted her seat belt and set her backpack on the floor of the car. "I don't know. I'm not really interested in seeing a bunch of naked guys strutting around like they're all that," she said.

"I know," Joanna agreed, relieved to find that she could probably count on

Lisa to stick by her if the others really did pursue 'adult entertainment.' Hoping to reinforce her ally, she added, "There is no bigger turn-off than a hot guy who thinks he's hot, or knows he's hot, and wants us to gush over him because he's hot."

***

The parking lot of Liberty High School was quite busy at five o'clock in the morning, on the day when the band and pom performers, teacher chaperones, and the band director, Mr. B, all gathered to board the coach bus that would transport them to the Minneapolis airport.

It was a crisp, clear morning, about twenty-six degrees, when Mrs. Conors drove Christopher and Joanna to school. "Well, here we are, my dears," she said cheerfully as she pulled into a parking space near the bus. She popped the trunk but kept the car running as she helped her children unload their luggage. "Soak up lots of sun for us... but make sure you wear your sunscreen!"

Christopher grabbed his backpack, his trumpet case, and his suitcase, and gave Mrs. Conors a quick hug. "Thanks, Mom!" He kissed her on the cheek.

Joanna grabbed her giant pom bag, her small airplane bag, and her suitcase. It was a challenge to fit everything she *thought* she'd need into one suitcase, but now was the time to learn the life skills of being practical and efficient. She hugged her mother and said, "Bye, Mom! I might not call at all, but if I do, will you accept the charges?"

Mrs. Conors chuckled. A long-distance phone call from Hawaii to Minnesota would be expensive, and she appreciated her daughter's conscientiousness about it. "Of course, Sweet Pea. You may call us anytime."

Sweet Pea. The nickname that her mother had given her when she was a baby stuck with her even to this day.

Mrs. Conors pulled Joanna close to her and kissed her on the cheek. "Have fun! And please! Wear your sunscreen! The rays are stronger over on those islands," she whispered into her ear.

"Yes, Mom!" Joanna groaned with a smile. It was hard to think about sunscreen right now, in the early morning dark, while their breath crystalized as they spoke. Joanna pulled her pink wool pompom snow hat off her head and tossed it to her mom. "Here, I'm not going to need this!" Mrs. Conors caught the hat and laughed.

Another car pulled up and Phebe and Lisa hopped out of it. Then many others arrived, and soon the bus was loaded and heading to the airport in Minneapolis.

***

The flight with fifty high school band students and ten pom squad performers was surprisingly mellow, and once they were airborne, Joanna sat back in her seat between Phebe and Lisa and smiled. "I can't wait to feel that warm sunshine," she said.

Phebe unbuckled her seat belt, and she knelt up in her place to look around. "I know we've been talking about this trip forever," she mused as she plopped back down into her seat. "But I can't believe this is finally it!"

"I know," Lisa agreed. "All those months of planning and talking about it..."

Joanna unbuckled her seat belt now and stood up to look around. She noticed a few rows in front of them, across the aisle, Nathan Hooks was sitting with his group from the popular crowd. Nathan was such a good-looking guy! The trombone player had dark hair and a nice smile, features that Joanna rarely got to see with him always sitting behind her in Homeroom. Joanna watched as he talked with his buddies nearby; they seemed to be goofing around with a deck of cards, but nothing obnoxious that bothered anyone.

Christopher was in the aisle seat across from them, and he leaned over to join in on the antics with the cards.

"You're drooling over Nathan again," Phebe teased her best friend, catching her stare. Right now, Joanna almost wished she had never confided in Phebe and Lisa that the one guy from the popular group that she would love to get to know was Nathan Hooks.

"I am not *drooling* over him," Joanna denied with a smile. "I'm just watching what he's doing with those cards, in case Christopher tries to..."

Phebe covered her mouth and fake-sneezed, while saying to the beat of her sneeze, "Bullshhmmp!"

Joanna giggled and said, "I love you too, Pheebs!"

"He's been looking over this way quite a bit, I've noticed," Lisa pointed out. "I think you should go for him, Jay. He's super smart. He was like the only one to get a hundred percent on that Economics test we had last week – and that one was a killer!"

"Yeah, and you are on his *list*, you know!" Phebe reminded her proudly.

"Yeah, that has not been confirmed, and I'm pretty sure that was a joke," Joanna muttered, and she plopped back into her seat. "I sit right in front of him in English class and all he's ever said to me was *What'd I miss?*." She remembered that exciting day, weeks ago. Sadly, that was the only time he had ever talked to her.

***

Anticipation of the islands peaked during the last stretch in flight, from Los Angeles to Honolulu, and the kids started to joke around about the floral necklace they would receive as they disembarked from the plane.

"Conors, we're gonna get *lei'd*!" Aaron Mickels called out loudly to Christopher.

Christopher raised his hands triumphantly in the air. "YESSS!"

"Hey Phebe!" Aaron now called over to the girls. "You wanna get *lei'd?*"

"Yeah, it's about dang time," Phebe muttered facetiously. Phebe was always good at quick retorts, no matter what was thrown at her.

Joanna giggled. She and her friends could joke about sexual things, which helped them to be 'cool' without compromising their values. But the truth was, they were all pretty innocent, unlike Pelin and her group, who probably really were planning to 'get laid.'

Soon the plane landed, and the passengers started to grab their carry-on bags from all the overhead bins. Matthew and Christopher were goofing around with Nicole and the others sitting near them, and suddenly Matthew called over to Joanna, "Hey, Jay! Someone over here wants to *lei* you!"

Nathan Hooks slapped Matthew playfully on the head and said, "Shut up, you *effer*!"

Matthew burst out laughing and Christopher said, "Hey! Don't talk about my big sister like that!"

Joanna called back, "Shut up over there!" Her cheeks burned slightly, but as she grabbed her bag, all she could think was... *Nathan Hooks!*

The cabin door opened and a set of steps was wheeled up to the plane. The students could smell the stunning floral aroma in the fresh Hawaiian air.

Flowers were everywhere! The morning sunshine, along with the balmy tropical humidity, seeped quickly into the plane's cabin. Everyone cheered and raved about the weather, and soon they disembarked, getting '*lei*-d.'

***

The bus ride to the hotel was rowdy until a tour guide held up a microphone and started telling everyone about the Hawaiian language, their alphabet, and how you could only purchase land or property on the islands if you are at least twenty-five percent native Hawaiian. Pelin Yilmaz declared that she might be "Hawaiian enough" to be able to purchase land if she wished.

Once the fascination of the beautiful blue-green ocean waters wore off during the forty-minute bus ride to the hotel, Joanna pulled her journal out of her bag and curled up against the window. Phebe was sitting next to her but was jabbering away with other friends in the nearby seats.

> We are in HAWAII, Herr Journal! Everything here smells like flowers, and everything is so bright and colorful! I got 'lei'd' when we got off the plane – ha ha, that was the big joke. But my lei is really pretty! I wonder how long it will last – it is made with <u>real</u> flowers. Pelin is already being annoying. For some reason, that girl just bugs me, and I hope she isn't going to be a thorn in my side this whole trip. Apparently, she's part Hawaiian. Or, at least she decided she was, once she found out that it is cool to be part Hawaiian. I'm pretty sure she's Turkish, but whatever.

When she was done writing, Joanna closed her journal and tossed it back into her bag. Lisa and Nicole were sitting behind her, and Lisa exclaimed, "Look, Joanna! Look at those palm trees!"

Matthew and Christopher, who were sitting in front of the girls, were also looking out the windows now. They were laughing about something someone else said, something about coconuts and that Aaron should stop talking about his nuts, and Matthew looked back at Joanna and Phebe. He just made a fake-shocked face and winked at them.

Chapter 9: Phebe's Secret

The Palm Residences hotel was an old thirty-five-story building sporting a rooftop pool, painfully slow elevators, and newly remodeled rooms. The students had spacious suites with an ocean view from the balcony, and a living area, small kitchen, a bathroom, and two or three bedrooms. The girls were on the 28th floor, and the 30th floor housed the boys.

Construction overtook the main entrance, and part of the east side of the building was blocked by orange cones and temporary safety fencing. Phebe noticed an overflowing trash can near a pile of cracked chunks of concrete. Two workers wearing hard hats and bright orange safety vests were jackhammering parts of the sidewalk.

Phebe groaned at the noise and said, "Wow. This is our hotel? We came all the way to Honolulu to stay in this crap-site?"

Lisa slapped Phebe's arm in an attempt to shush her. "Phebe! Don't start insulting everything already!"

"This is nice!" Joanna exclaimed, once they got inside the lobby. "Look at that little waterfall. And I LOVE how open this all is! No walls closing up everything and blocking out all the daylight!"

"I wonder if we'll find a *taboo*," Phebe mused facetiously, referencing an episode from one of their favorite TV shows. Joanna and Lisa giggled at their inside joke.

Joanna, Phebe, Lisa, and Nicole were assigned to room 2806, a suite for four. Christopher, Matthew, Aaron, Nathan, Colvin, and Grant were up in a six-person suite, room 3002. There was an outdoor buffet that was open 24 hours just across the street from the back of the Palm Residences hotel, where the group planned to eat most of their meals.

Once everyone got checked into their rooms, the students were free to do whatever they wished for the rest of the day. They were reminded of the rules: curfew was midnight every night, and they must be rested and ready for all performances. They were given a schedule of all the performances for the week, with the times they were expected to be outside and ready for the bus. They had maps of the Waikiki Beach strip, and were required to get permission from a chaperone before going on any excursions. They were advised to stay in small groups, and absolutely forbidden to go anywhere alone. There were "ABC" convenience stores on every corner where they could buy groceries or snacks.

"I can't believe it's only one o'clock in the afternoon!" Lisa yawned as she wheeled her suitcase into the bedroom that she and Phebe would share for the week. Normally in a situation like this, Joanna and Phebe would be the ones to share a room, but Joanna, Lisa, and Phebe had been best friends with each other since kindergarten, and Nicole had only joined 'the group' this school year since she was dating Christopher. Nicole felt most comfortable with Joanna, so she had asked Joanna to be her roommate while they were on this trip.

Nicole was very pretty. She had long dark hair that she sometimes curled with big bouncy waves, and other times blow-dried out to be stick-straight. She had big, dark blue eyes and a clear complexion, with three modest moles placed just right on her face, so that they enhanced, rather than detracted from, her beauty. Her ears were double-pierced, and she always wore hoop earrings in the first holes. Her body was similar to Joanna's – tall and slender – but she had a chest that was much fuller than what Joanna could ever hope for.

"I know," Nicole agreed. "It's, like, six o'clock at home. I'm exhausted!"

"Me too. I'm taking a nap," Lisa announced, and she fell onto her twin bed.

Joanna and Phebe were hungry, so they changed into their shorts, tank tops, and sandals, and they headed outside to explore and look for something to eat. They couldn't find anyone else from the trip that they wanted to hang out with, so they just walked together along the sidewalk to take in all the beauty, and see what the food options were.

"Do we have to get normal food?" Joanna wondered, as she eyed up an ice cream shop on the corner. A woman stepped outside holding a wad of napkins surrounding a giant waffle cone with creamy peppermint chocolate chip ice cream dripping from it. "Or can we get one of those?"

"I think we can get whatever we want," Phebe replied. "We should probably get real food, but let's get ice cream anyway!" She pulled Joanna inside.

The girls got their cones and then found a bench on the sidewalk, where pasty white sand met the concrete. The sidewalk led all the way along the waterfront. "So, is this, like, *the* beach?" Phebe wondered aloud.

Joanna kicked off her sandals and dug her newly painted bright-pink toes into the warm, soft, white grains. "Yeah, I think so. A little different than the one at Lake W, huh?" The large body of water in Woodland Hills was known only as "Lake W."

"Look at that!" Phebe marveled, pushing her sunglasses to the top of her head to be sure she was really seeing what she was seeing. "The beach just goes on and on and... on and on!"

"Yeah. And so does the ocean!" Joanna added. "I need to start taking some pictures when I finish this cone!"

The girls found a bench to sit on, and they ate their ice cream quickly to keep up with the melting. Then Phebe sighed, and took a deep, dramatic breath. "Okay, so... Jay... Ughh! I have to tell someone! But you can't tell anyone! Swear?"

Joanna smiled and caught another drip of her ice cream. Phebe always had things that she "has to tell someone," and Joanna was always promising not to tell anyone. And she never did. Joanna was the most trustworthy friend when it came to 'secrets,' along with Lisa. The three girls had been sharing everything with each other since about fifth grade, when they started to have girly things to share with each other. "Swear," Joanna confirmed, holding up her pinky finger. She couldn't imagine what the secret was this time.

Phebe's dark greenish-brown eyes sparkled as she turned to Joanna and said with a hint of uncertainty, "I like Matthew. I think."

Joanna almost dropped her drippy cone, and her brain raced to translate what she just heard. She couldn't stop herself from exclaiming, "What?!"

Joanna was not expecting anything like this. She was not ready for this! Matthew had been Christopher's best friend since just about the day they were born, which, by default, had made Joanna almost a best friend to him too. If nothing else, Joanna and Matthew were best-friendier with each other more so than any other given boy/girl pair in their group.

But they were all *friends*. Nobody within that group was supposed to be 'liking' each other!

"I know!" Phebe groaned happily. Her eyes fluttered toward the clear blue sky. "*I know* this is weird because you're, like, his best female friend, but that's why I'm confiding this in you! Because you know him best. I need a boyfriend. It's time for me to have a boyfriend, and he's so funny and the most fun of all the guys, so... I don't know. I think I like him."

"So, you want him to be your *boyfriend*?" Joanna asked, trying to clarify whatever she was hearing. She ignored the thick, creamy slop of her cookies-n-cream ice cream that was now dripping down the side of her hand.

Phebe shrugged and licked her own chocolate ice cream to keep it from dripping. "I don't know. Maybe I don't like *him*, really."

"But you want a boyfriend," Joanna stated, forcing confidence into her tone.

"Well... yes."

Joanna relaxed somewhat, and returned to the maintenance of the drips from her ice cream. She reiterated, "So you want a boyfriend. And since nobody else seems that desirable, you think you should ask Matthew out?"

Phebe thought for a moment. "Hmmm. Well, no, not really, I guess. He's just so cool, though."

"Oh Pheebs," Joanna sighed, putting her arm around her best friend. "Here we are in Hawaii, so you are falling into the grips of the desire for romance."

"Well, what about you?" Phebe said. "If you go for Nathan Hooks, then I have to find *someone*!"

"Nathan Hooks!" Joanna exclaimed. "I'm not going for Na—"

"Ohhh, nice try, JC!" Phebe laughed. "This is the perfect time to make him realize who he's sittin' behind in his homeroom. You should ask him out!"

Joanna giggled. "He *is* cute. But he would have to ask *me* out, not the other way around. I'm a traditional girl."

"Well, maybe he will!" Phebe suggested. "He was lookin' at us during all that traveling..."

"Ohhhhh, I wish... Can you even imagine??" Joanna caught the last drips of her ice cream out of the bottom of the cone, and then stuffed what was left of the pointed end into her mouth.

The girls started walking again. As they began their search for real food, they came across a Jack-of-all-Trades.

"Jack-of-all-Trades!" Phebe exclaimed when they saw the sign for the fast-food place near its entrance. Woodland Hills didn't have a Jack-of-all-Trades, but the girls had heard of it. The building was made of brick, with a giant red cube at the top. The paint on all of the outdoor patio's cheap picnic tables was chipped, and a stand-alone menu board boasted a life-size mascot:

a character with a head that looked like a softball with eyes and a mouth, standing in a clown suit.

The girls looked at the menu: burgers and fries in every form imaginable. "What kind of name is *Jack-of-all-Trades* for a restaurant?" Phebe demanded. "That name implies one of everything. But they only have burgers!"

"This mascot is creepy," Joanna said, looking at the mortared smile on the pasty-white softball head, atop the clown suit. "And the name is probably because they have one of every kind of *burger* imaginable."

"Jack*off*-of-all-Trades. That's what I'm going to call it," Phebe decided firmly.

Joanna rolled her eyes, although nothing about Phebe's comment was surprising. That was just Phebe!

When the girls returned to their 'crap-site' hotel that afternoon, Phebe commented that she was feeling kind of lonely now. Lisa and Nicole were both gone. "Where is everyone? We don't have anyone to talk to!" she cried.

Joanna was rather enjoying the break from the hustle and bustle they had experienced all morning, so she just shrugged, and they started looking through the schedule and some of the brochures that were on the coffee table. Then Joanna giggled, and said something about how when this trip first came about, back in September, her dad wanted to be one of the chaperones. "Christopher and I were both like, *No way!*"

"Awww," Phebe said wistfully. "I wish your dad was here right now."

Joanna looked at her, confused. "You do? Why?" Phebe had liked Joanna's parents when they were kids, but as teenagers, Phebe didn't really like any parents. Mr. Conors was a very pleasant guy, however, and he had a good rapport with his children's friends.

"Because then we'd have someone to talk to!"

Joanna giggled again and stood up. She grabbed the phone and said, "I'm going to call my family right now." Then she paused and looked at the little card near the phone. "As soon as I... figure out how to dial long distance."

"That's going to cost a fortune," Phebe warned her. "My mom told me not to call, no matter what! She said it's too expensive."

Joanna knew that it would be expensive, but her parents wouldn't make a deal of it this one time.

When Joanna's mother answered, Phebe yelled from the background, "Hi Mrs. Conors! Tell my mom I'm safe and having fun because she won't let me call her!"

Mrs. Conors chuckled and said to Joanna, "How're you doing, Sweet Pea?" Joanna told her about the ice cream and the white sand and the warm, sunny weather, and how everything smelled like flowers. Then when Mr. Conors got on the phone, he said proudly, "Well, Joanna-Bear, I won the bet."

"What was the bet?"

"The bet was, *Will Joanna call this week?* Mom said no way, but I said yes, of course she will," he told her.

Joanna giggled. "Well, I just wanted to say hi." Then she heard her mother say in the background, "Christopher won't call though, that one I'm most sure of!"

"Is your brother staying out of trouble so far?" Mr. Conors asked Joanna.

"Yeah, so far! I don't know where he is now, though, or what he's doing. Everyone disappeared, and Phebe and I got lonely, so we decided to call you."

"Well good," Mr. Conors said, amused. "I'm glad that when everyone else on the trip has abandoned you, you realize your ol' mom and dad are good for something."

Hawaii is already becoming an adventure, Herr Journal. The air is so tropical and warm... But let me just cut to the chase: Phebe confided in me that she likes Matthew!! Matthew, OUR Matthew, Herr Journal! What am I supposed to say to that? Hello! We are not supposed to be liking each other in our friend group! I've never thought about this before, and now it bothers me that she likes him. What if he likes her back? I don't know... this is kind of unsettling to me....

Chapter 10: Party Cruise

Almost everyone spent the whole next day on the beach, soaking up the rays of the beautiful, warm Hawaiian sun. But they soaked up a bit more than they should have, and by early afternoon, the Minnesotans were starting to look painfully red.

"They probably sell some aloe or something at that ABC store," Lisa suggested, as the group gathered their towels and bags to head back to the hotel.

"Yeah, let's check out the ABC store!" Phebe exclaimed, as Joanna asked them which one they'd want to go to. The girls were curious about these ABC stores: These small convenience stores sold snacks, toiletries, and souvenirs, and there seemed to be one on just about every street corner.

The girls entered the next one they saw, and while they were looking for their aloe, Phebe pointed out a display of condoms. "Two dollars and sixty-nine cents!" she whispered with exasperation. "Nice way to set the price. Two people, sixty-nining..." She grabbed a package to study it more closely.

Joanna rolled her eyes. The sign by the display read, *For when the time is right...* "You know, you wouldn't need those if you're just sixty-nining," she pointed out.

Phebe put the package she was holding back on the shelf and said, "Well, you never know when *the time will be right*, Jay." Lisa giggled.

"The strap on my bag is hurting my tender shoulders," Joanna complained. "Let's get this aloe and go."

***

There was a knock at the door of suite 2806 that night, and when Lisa answered it, Pelin and Dana burst into the room. "We're going to try to find the Hard Rock Café for dinner," they announced. "You guys want to come with us?"

It seemed a little odd that suddenly Pelin and Dana were inviting middle-class girls to hang out. Though the pom squad didn't recognize social order, that idea usually only held up at games or official school events. But the girls agreed to go along, thinking this may be a chance for the upper crusters to see that the middle-class girls weren't so bad after all.

Pelin and Dana led Joanna, Phebe, Lisa, Nicole, and a couple of others down the boardwalk in search of the restaurant, when they were approached by a young man and woman. The couple introduced themselves as "Boris and Lucille," and they spoke with British accents.

"Have you heard of the Party Cruise?" Lucille asked them, in her thick British accent. She had a collared white shirt on, with a colorful logo embroidered near her shoulder that read *Party Cruise*.

Right then, Joanna's heart began to race. She became nervous, but the others were sucked in. The word "party" was one that often created anxiety for Joanna, and hearing it here in Hawaii was no exception. At this age, in high school, "party" meant unsupervised drinking and possibly drugs, as well as other things that Joanna did not want to be part of.

The Party Cruise was a boat cruise where only young people were allowed on, Lucille explained, and they could drink as much as they want, "safely," all night. Joanna's jaw dropped as these two *adults* promised to get all these minors drunk if they came on the cruise!

"Is this even legal??" Joanna whispered to Lisa, hoping that she'd still be her ally when it came to this moral equivocation. Phebe and the others were listening intently, as Lucille gave them information not only about how to get on the Party Cruise, but also how to get fake IDs made, and how they could get into Seely's Strip Bar with drinks all night. Boris winked at Pelin, who was all over this idea.

"You guys!" Pelin exclaimed, once Lucille and Boris had moved on. She swung her long dark hair dramatically over her shoulder. "This is so awesome! We can do the Party Cruise tonight..."

Dana piped in with how they would cover for each other to meet curfew, even if they were drunk. Nicole played it cool and didn't say anything one way or another, and Phebe offered that she was probably not going to do the Party Cruise that night, but she'd join them for the strip club later in the week. Phebe was good at that – talking the talk but postponing the walk.

"I can't believe those two *adults* were out soliciting minors, promising to get us drunk!" Joanna muttered disgustedly later when she, Phebe, and Lisa headed back to their hotel. Nicole met up with Christopher, as they had their own plans for the evening.

"That is odd," Lisa added thoughtfully. "I wonder how they can get away with that?"

"I think it sounds pretty cool," Phebe said. Her ruby-red sunburned cheeks reflected the last rays of that evening's setting sun.

"Yeah, well they probably set up undercover cops and it's a trap," Joanna hoped aloud. Her own sunburned cheeks hurt when she talked.

"Oh, it's not going to be a trap," Phebe snapped impatiently. "You gotta live it up a little, Jay. We're in Hawaii! Besides, if you don't go, you'll probably be the only one who doesn't."

"Good. I can live with being the only one not putting myself into all these compromising situations."

Phebe rolled her eyes, but Joanna didn't care. She was still in shock that a grown man and woman, a married couple, who presumably had their own young children, or would someday, were out leading young, impressionable, foolish teenagers on a path to moral destruction.

It was that night that Joanna decided she would become a nun.

***

There was an informal trivia game going on in the lobby of the Palm Residences hotel that evening. Knowing that it would take forever for their elevator to come, Joanna and Phebe plopped their exhausted bodies down on a couch to hang out for a while.

The trivia moderator spoke into a microphone to the growing audience, his voice dominating the lobby. "And... We have another geography question," he said. "Name the second largest country in South America." Despite all the construction outside, this area was well-groomed with open walls, cushioned seating around cased-in tropical plants, and two small waterfalls trickling in the background.

Phebe picked up a giant Alocasia leaf that was lying on the couch cushion near her and rubbed it gently between her fingers. "South America..." she mused as she stroked the spine of the leaf. "Brazil would be the largest country, I know that. But I don't know what the second-largest country would be."

"It's Argentina," Joanna said, as she turned her arm to try to see her elbow. "Ow! My face hurts to talk!"

Christopher, Matthew, and a few others walked by then, just as the moderator confirmed Argentina to be the second-largest country in South America. Joanna clapped her hands together delightfully and cheered, "Ohhh yeah! I am the geography queen!"

Christopher went over to his sister and sat next to her, greeting her with a cheerful, "Hi, Lobster!"

Falling against the back of the couch again, Joanna's arms sprawled out at her sides, and her legs dangled off the cushions. She was wearing a loose cotton t-shirt and loose cotton shorts, and she looked terribly uncomfortable.

The trivia moderator went on with his next question, "What US city is home to the Gateway Arch?"

"Oh lordy-be!" Joanna moaned, looking in the direction of the trivia leader and almost sounding disappointed. "These are so easy! St. Louis!" Then she turned to her brother. Anticipating his curiosity, she started to explain with a tone of boredom, "I thought my sunblock was in my bag when we went down to the beach." This would be the third time she had to tell her story to all the curious friends who had come by, and for her, it was tremendously uninteresting. "It wasn't, and I was too lazy to walk *allllll* the way back to the hotel and wait for the dang elevator that would have taken about eight hours to come, so I borrowed some lotion from Pelin, because I liked the smell of hers better than Phebe's, but Pelin's was actually tanning *accelerator*, not sunblock. So here I am."

Christopher and Matthew laughed, and Christopher gently slapped her leg.

"Ouch!" she shrieked, jumping up and whacking her brother on the arm. "Don't touch my delicate skin!"

Aaron Mickels came over to the group then and joked with the girls about their sunburn. Joanna's was definitely the worst, but Phebe's and Lisa's weren't far behind. Aaron smiled devilishly and teased Joanna, "Awww... Nate-Dog will never recognize you like this! He thinks he's chasing a Caucasian girl!"

His teasing continued, and since Phebe wanted to see Joanna and Nathan get together, she joined in on the razzing.

Joanna still didn't believe that Nathan even knew who she was, let alone would like her, and she became embarrassed as things started to blow out of proportion. She kept nudging Phebe to stop, and when Phebe didn't, Joanna finally stood up and said loudly, "Matthew, I have something to tell you. Come here."

Phebe's teasing came to an immediate halt; she looked, startled, at Joanna. Her eyes were frantic, then pleading. Joanna shot back at her with seriousness, her own bright blue-green eyes silently, but clearly, proclaiming, *Two can play at this game, my friend!*

Matthew stood up and went curiously over to Joanna, and Joanna looked again at Phebe's desperately pleading eyes.

Rapid contemplation of how Phebe could definitely push the limits consumed Joanna for a brief moment. Though it wasn't very often, Phebe could be annoying, and she didn't always stop when enough was enough. But Phebe was still Joanna's best friend. And the rest of the trip would be awfully long if the two of them were fighting.

Joanna waited a moment – a moment that must have seemed like an eternity to Phebe – but then turned to Matthew and said, "Never mind. I don't have anything to tell you."

So much is happening, Herr Journal!! Everyone's been teasing me about that really popular kid, Nathan Hooks... I don't know what the deal is with that, but he is one of the hottest guys in that group... I almost betrayed Phebe by telling Matthew that she likes him, because she was being kind of a turd tonight. I'm using the word 'turd' because I don't really want to call my best friend a total B-word, but in all honestly, the B-word would probably be a more accurate description.

Anyway, I was about to betray Phebe but then I thought better of it and kept my mouth shut. I'm afraid to find out if Matthew might like her back!

OH! And get this: these GROWN ADULTS came up to us and tried to sell us tickets to a party cruise, where they promised to get us all drunk... all of us MINORS! I don't even know what to think about that, but Pelin, of course, was all for this idea.

Chapter 11: Luau Romance

The group's first performance in Hawaii would take place at Bishop Square on Sunday, and now the rumor was that Aaron Mickels liked Phebe. As they rode the bus to the performance site, Joanna said to her best friend, "They're all saying Aaron likes you. Are you going to go out with him if he asks you out?"

Phebe smiled. "Yeah! I'd probably go out with him." She tried to play it cool, but excitement was bursting from her eyes. Her medium brown curls bounced loosely around her face.

Joanna breathed a sigh of relief, and she relaxed in her seat as the bus jostled down the bumpy road. She wasn't keen on the idea of Phebe liking Matthew, but Phebe liking Aaron Mickels would be okay.

They arrived at the small amphitheater, and once everyone was ready and waiting for their turn to perform, Christopher came over to Joanna. She was sitting by herself on a small rock bench that enclosed a palm tree. "Mickels likes Pheebs," he said, rubbing the side of his trumpet with the fabric of his shirt.

"Yeah, so I hear!" she replied. "She likes him too, so tell him to ask her out." *The sooner we can set this in stone, the better*, she thought.

"Rumor has it that Nathan Hooks wants to ask you out," he told her. Christopher was always a bit protective of his sister, and until this year, he never had to worry about guys wanting to date her because she was never interested. But now, he sensed that she might be interested, and his brotherly protectiveness was kicking in.

Joanna smiled and looked off to the side. "Hmmm. Well, he seems like a nice fellow." She pulled her knee up to tie a double knot in one of her shoes.

"A nice *fellow*?" Christopher repeated. "What are we, in England?"

"Yeah. I'm sure he's a nice fellow."

"Well, that'd be fun, Jo-Jo. You and he could go out with me and Nicole, like on a double-date!" Christopher always liked doing social things with his twin.

Joanna stood up and grabbed her pompoms. "Well, one thing at a time, Big Brother. The guy sits behind me in Homeroom/English class, and he never talks to me. So, we could almost say, technically, we haven't even officially met."

***

That evening there was a Luau planned for all the students, scheduled for sunset. Phebe was sitting next to Joanna on the bus, but before the bus departed, she stood up and disappeared. A moment later, Nathan Hooks appeared, and sat down next to Joanna.

"Oh!" Joanna said simply, and she looked at him. The scent of his Calvin Klein *Obsession for Men* engulfed her, and her heartrate sped up. His arm brushed against hers, and she uttered, "I... I think Phebe is sitting here."

"Nah," said Nathan, smoothing out a wrinkle in his khaki shorts. "She wanted to sit next to Aaron. I guess they're goin' out now." Then he turned to Joanna and extended his hand. "I'm Nathan, by the way. Do you mind if I sit here? Since I lost my seat to your friend?"

Joanna smiled and shook his hand politely. "Hi Nathan, I'm Joanna. Sure, you can sit here."

"Thanks," he smiled back, and Joanna noticed that one of his front teeth was slightly turned in front of the other. Not in a crooked or ugly way, but it was just something she noticed. She liked his smile. "So, you're Christopher's sister," he went on then, trying to make conversation.

"Yep! We're twins," she told him. "Guess which one of us is older."

"Hmmm," he thought for a moment. "You're way prettier than he is, so I'll guess that you were born first."

Joanna giggled and asked, "What do looks have to do with birth order?" She noticed his eyes were a very solid, medium blue color, surrounded by a nice set of dark eyelashes that any woman would kill for.

Nathan shrugged. "I don't know. I was just trying to give you a compliment. I guess that didn't make sense!"

"Well, you're very sweet," Joanna told him. "And you are correct: I was born first. But I call him *Big Brother* because he's taller than me now."

The ride to the luau was rather long, and after the initial small talk, Nathan took Joanna's hand and held it on his leg. Joanna found this gesture to be rather bold, since she had only officially met him minutes earlier, but she didn't mind it. His hand was strong and soft, and hers fit nicely in it. "You have pretty hands," he said, attempting another compliment. "Are these your real fingernails?"

Joanna gave him a funny look. She didn't think there was anything remarkable about her fingernails; they came just past the tips of her fingers, and were painted hot pink to match her toes. Nothing fancy. "My real fingernails? That's kind of an odd thing to say to a girl, isn't it?"

Nathan chuckled uneasily and fumbled, "Oh, I don't know! Don't all you girls go to the salons and get your nails done and all that?"

This guy is super nervous! Joanna concluded quietly inside her head, realizing now his struggle to make conversation. *This is unbelievable! Mr. Popular is talking to me, and HE is nervous!* So, she looked at him and said matter-of-factly, "There is *nothing* fake about me, Nathan. What you see is what you get." She winked at him and tried to hide a smile, which revealed the dimple in her left cheek.

Nathan relaxed slightly, and recovered with, "Oh. Well, I guess I was just trying to compliment you again."

It was on this night that Joanna decided she would *not* become a nun!

Nathan was very attentive to Joanna at the luau. They made real flower bracelets, and Nathan ended up on the stage. Thanks to his buddies, who volunteered him as a hula dancer, he made quite a show of clumsily swaying his body in all directions. Joanna giggled as Nathan tried to keep a beat with the ukuleles and xaphoons played by the luau staff.

Noticing how entertaining Joanna found Nathan to be, Aaron Mickels started making wisecrack comments to Joanna, like, "Boy, Nathan sure has a nice butt, don't you think so, Joanna? Look at his butt! Isn't it nice?" This was annoying, and it confirmed to Joanna why she never wanted to be in the spotlight when it came to dating.

Nathan held Joanna's hand again as they strolled around the luau. She liked it, and it was very comfortable, but she also couldn't help worrying what others might be thinking. High schoolers love matchmaking their friends. *What if Christopher sees me holding hands with this guy? Are all of Nathan's friends speculating things? Are the popular girls annoyed that Mr. Popular is holding hands with a middle-class girl?* So much social pressure!

As they sauntered along in the sand, Aaron Mickels made another wisecrack towards Joanna and Nathan about Nathan's butt, so Joanna said to Nathan, "I think Aaron is nervous about 'dating' Phebe. He's being kind of obnoxious."

Nathan laughed. "Maybe *I* should be concerned that he is analyzing my butt!"

There was a modest buffet of cheap food presented for the guests, and after eating a small plateful of pineapple, strawberries, and little skewered chicken bites, Nathan asked Joanna if she wanted to go look at the sunset. "It's gettin' to be that time, I think. I hear the sunsets in Hawaii are phenomenal."

The sidewalk along the sandy beach was lined with trees full of white blossoms, and the sweet fragrance of the flowers mesmerized Joanna. This minor distraction from what was happening with Nathan was what she needed while the evening wore on. "Mmmm..." she breathed in the intense aroma as Nathan squeezed her hand gently. "This is so amazing!" She pulled her hand away momentarily to point to the tree branches above them. "Everywhere we go, we can smell these beautiful flowers."

Nathan took her hand again. "I know! It *is* amazing."

He led her across the sand, where several boulders stood against the calm waves that were crawling to the shore. Music from the luau could be heard from just a short distance away, and the deep rays of the sun were dropping lower on the horizon. Nathan put his arm around her, and they sat on the rocks. *This is unbelievable,* Joanna pondered inside her head once again. *I never talked to this guy but once throughout our entire high school career together, and now Mr. Popular, Mr. GQ, is holding my hand! I have a feeling I know where this is going...*

They talked about how beautiful the sunset was, and Nathan told her how beautiful she was. He told her how beautiful her hair was. *He's going to kiss me,* Joanna realized inside her head. *It's only a matter of time now...*

Joanna had never kissed anyone before. Not on the lips, anyway. Well, she *sort of* had been kissed in eighth grade, when Matthew took her to the Middle School Mixer and *sort of* kissed her on the side of her mouth. The two of them had considered it to be an "experiment," or a practice. They never did it again, they never talked about it, and they never told anyone about it. Joanna never really decided whether she considered that to be her first kiss.

But now... Now, Nathan brushed her hair aside and whispered again in her ear how beautiful she was. She contemplated whether she wanted this to happen, because it was indeed happening! *I'm going to have my first real kiss, right here on the beach before this beautiful sunset in beautiful Hawaii, with this really hot guy in the popular group named Nathan. This is incredible!*

Nathan's head was touching hers now, although she was still facing her hands in her lap. But then, she decided, it was time. She slowly lifted her face toward his, and she let him kiss her.

Joanna was surprised to find this kiss to be more than just a little peck. It was squishy, and she could feel his tongue moving around. It seemed like a pretty long kiss to her, but she really didn't have a frame of reference to support that thought. Finally, she pulled away a little bit and just looked into his nice, solid blue eyes. Her heart was racing, and her mind was too. *My very first kiss! A tongue kiss! I don't even know this kid, and I just let him stick his tongue into my mouth!* Her hands were shaking a little bit now too, and when she could feel Nathan moving close to her again, she said, "We should probably go back to our table. These rocks are poking into my butt!"

As they walked back to the luau area, which was now intimately lit with tiki torches, Joanna noticed that her lips were wettish, but really dried out. They felt very chapped.

She carefully sat down next to Nicole at a table. *Are people looking at us?* she wondered silently. Phebe and Lisa, along with about a million other people, were all up on a stage platform learning a hula dance, and the tour guide, "Cousin Tom," was trying to teach them simple choreography. Nathan had gone over to meet up with the guys at another table.

"So, what happened?" Nicole asked her. "You guys were gone for a while..."

Joanna turned to her brother's girlfriend and said, "Now I know why you always need ChapStick after seeing Christopher."

Nicole grabbed Joanna's arm and said excitedly, "Really?!"

Joanna smiled and nodded.

"So..." Nicole looked at her, trying to get more information. But Joanna didn't have any more information.

Word spread quickly to Phebe and Lisa once they returned from their hula lesson. "Well, what about you and Aaron?" Joanna demanded, trying to take the attention off of herself. "What's up with that?" She really wished she'd brought her lip balm along.

"He asked me out, so we're going out, I guess!" Phebe bragged happily.

"Well, what's *going out*?" Joanna asked her. "Like, is he your *boyfriend* now?"

"Yeah, I guess! He kissed me over there under those trees by that statue thing."

"Boy, what a night!" Lisa exclaimed. "Where's a man for me?"

Joanna didn't talk to Nathan for the rest of the night, however. She *sort of* avoided him, but he stayed with the guys anyway, so it was a non-issue. She asked Lisa to just 'happen' to sit with her on the bus ride back to the hotel. "I'm not sure how I feel about Nathan," she confessed to Lisa quietly during the ride. "I'm sort of freaked out that he kissed me."

"Well, what did you think he would do, while you were alone together out there by the sunset on the shores of the Pacific Ocean?" Lisa asked her with a smile.

"Yeah, I guess," Joanna admitted. "But I always thought my first kiss would be when I'm head over heels in love, and it would *finally* happen after me wanting a kiss so badly. This all happened so fast! I don't even really know what happened!"

Lisa smiled. She had been kissed only once, the previous summer, during a co-ed summer camp activity where a kid from northern Wisconsin liked her. She never saw him again after that camp. "Well, instead, your first kiss was on the shores of Hawaii. Not too many people can say that."

"But is that bad?" Joanna asked Lisa, almost in a panic. "I mean... I'm not in love with the guy! And kissing leads to other things..."

"Ohhhh Joanna," Lisa sighed compassionately, and she rested her head on her friend's shoulder. "You're so funny. You can kiss a guy, even if you aren't sure yet if you really like him."

"Well, I don't want to send the wrong message!"

"Oh my goodness!" Lisa laughed. Joanna was *so* innocent. Not naïve, but just so sweet and innocent.

"And anyway, he's Mr. GQ in the popular group. Don't you think it's a little odd that he's stepping down to our level for a kiss?"

"Well, Joanna, you *are* pretty, and nice. And maybe he's not as superficial as everyone else in that group. Or maybe it doesn't matter, because you're a pom girl, and maybe they're allowed to date pom girls."

"Hmmm. Well, it seems a little too good to be true."

***

The phone rang in suite 2806 later that night, when everyone was back at the hotel and getting ready for bed. Matthew was calling to talk to Joanna.

Lisa and Phebe closed their door and went to bed. Nicole also went into the other bedroom and closed the door. Everyone was exhausted, but Joanna curled up in her pajamas on the couch in the living area to take her phone call.

"So.... What's up with Nathan?" Matthew asked her sensitively. It was not a nosy question, and it wasn't piggish. It was just a friendly question that was totally normal in their *Freundschaft*.

"Why do you want to know?" Joanna asked him sweetly. She had been close with Matthew since the beginning of time, and she would have had no problem talking about this with him. But right now, she herself didn't even know what was up with Nathan, so she wasn't sure how to answer his question. She bought herself some time with her own question, and hoped that maybe Matthew had some information from Nathan's end.

"I'm just curious," Matthew said softly.

Joanna sighed. She could tell that Matthew was trying to talk quietly even though there seemed to be commotion in his room. Clearly his roommates were not headed for bed anytime soon.

"It's pretty noisy up there," she commented.

"Yeah... Ughh," he groaned. "I want to talk to you, Jay. Can you come down to the lobby?"

Joanna looked at her pajama shorts, tank top, and sunburned legs, and, after checking the clock, she said, "It's curfew in ten minutes. If Mr. B catches us in the lobby, we'll be toast, and we'll never get back in time with that stupid elevator. Why don't you come down to our room quick? Use the stairwell. We can talk here. Everyone went to bed."

A moment later, there was a soft tap on the door, and Joanna let Matthew in. She had pulled on her new light-pink Waikiki Beach hoodie over her tank top to maintain her modesty.

"I don't really know what's going on with Nathan," she admitted quietly when they sat down. She rested her arm and chin against the wide side of the armchair where she was now sitting, then she looked at Matthew on the couch across from her. "I mean, he's not in our league. He's wayyyyyy above us, so I don't get why he's stepping down like this. But he's been super nice and sweet and ...."

Matthew said cautiously, very quietly, "And he *kissed* you?"

"How'd you know that?" Joanna asked him, although she already had a good idea. Phebe could be such a blab!

Matthew told her that Aaron saw them, and Phebe confirmed it later, or something. He couldn't really remember how he knew, he just knew.

"I guess I was just caught off-guard," Joanna admitted. "I wasn't really expecting *that* right away, since we really don't know each other that well."

"Yeah, I understand," Matthew nodded. Then he asked, "So, is he a good kisser?"

Joanna extended her leg out, as if she would kick him playfully, and smiled. "That's none of your business, and that's not the point!" she said.

Matthew laughed. "I'm just kidding, Jay."

There was a pause, and then Joanna said, "Matthew, you don't think this is a joke, do you?"

"A joke?" He looked confused.

"Yeah. Like, a prank. Like, *let's get Mr. GQ to pretend to like the boring ol' middle-class girl and see if she falls for it, and...* You know, just to mess with me or whatever?"

Matthew sat up straight now and became serious. "No. No, Jay, not at all. That's why I wanted to talk to you. The word on the street up there is that he really genuinely does like you... and he's worried that you don't really like him!"

"I guess... well, I guess I've always thought he was cute," she went on. "But I never in a million years imagined that someone so popular would like me!"

Matthew nodded in thought.

Then Joanna confided, "And... I've never really liked anyone before. So now that I kind of do, I just assumed he wouldn't like me back. And if it's true that he does, I don't really know what to do with that!"

Matthew burst into a slight laugh. Joanna was a very pretty girl, and it was only a matter of time before other guys started to notice this. Even the popular guys.

They were both quiet for a moment, and then Matthew changed the subject. "What were you going to tell me in the lobby the other day?"

Oops.

Joanna regretted now having hinted something to him, and she had hoped Matthew wouldn't follow up. "Um... I can't tell you," she said.

"What do you mean you can't tell me?"

Joanna looked around their quiet suite. The bedroom doors were closed and everyone else was presumably asleep. Even so, she couldn't betray her best friend, nor could she trust there was any true privacy in this "crap-site" hotel.

But does it matter now, anyway? she thought. *Supposedly Phebe is dating Aaron, so the Matthew-crush is a non-factor, right?* Still, Joanna didn't like the idea of Phebe liking Matthew, and she wanted to find out if there were any feelings on Matthew's end. *After all, we might be back in this boat again if the thing with Aaron doesn't work out!*

"I can't tell you, Matthew," she maintained, but she caught his eye and added directly, "I can't betray *the trust of my best friend, Phebe.*" She added that she is *sworn to secrecy.* "Let's just say that what I was going to tell you earlier shouldn't matter anymore *now*, since Phebe *likes _Aaron_ now. Instead.*" Her emphasis on the word *instead* was firm and confident, and she maintained the connection with her eyes.

Matthew caught on quickly at that. "She liked *me*?" he whispered, suddenly looking uncomfortable.

Joanna didn't say anything more, and Matthew just sat in thought. Finally, he turned to Joanna and said weakly, "Oh Joanna, please. Please don't let her like me. And please don't repeat this... but between me and you... I mean, Phebe is fun and all, and I know she's your BFF and all that, but..." he shook his head and made a face, clearly unable to say in words that he was not at all interested in Phebe in any way.

Joanna silently breathed a sigh of relief, and assured Matthew that probably he needn't worry since Phebe was with Aaron.

Matthew looked at the clock then, and stood up. "I'd better get back to my room. Thanks for the chat, Jay." He gave Joanna a quick hug, and she walked him to the door.

When they opened the door to the hallway, Matthew nearly smacked right into Mr. B, the band director, who was walking through the hallway checking curfew. Joanna was right behind Matthew, having just patted him on the shoulder as she was saying good-bye. None of this looked good to their chaperone.

"Mr. Carmichael!" Mr. B exclaimed in surprise. He looked at his watch. "It is 12:08 AM, young man, and I believe we have a rule about you guys not being on this floor."

Matthew stood straight and cleared his throat confidently. "Yes sir, Mr. B. Yes. Um... You see, well, Christopher had a little bag in his suitcase that belonged to Joanna, and she needed it tonight." Then Matthew lowered his voice to a whisper and said awkwardly, "It was a bag of... girl stuff... if you know what I mean, Sir."

Mr. B squirmed now a bit, and Matthew went on, "So anyways, Christopher for some reason had to shove it in his suitcase last minute as they were leaving home and Joanna needed it... like... *now*, and Christopher was asleep and... well, I just thought I could run it down here quickly for her."

Mr. B was an older gentleman who had raised six children with his wife of thirty years, and he understood family dynamics. He also didn't want to know anything more about 'girl stuff.' He certainly found Matthew's story plausible, and Matthew, Joanna, and Christopher were on his private mental list of 'good kids,' so he let this one go, with just a kindly warning.

What a day, Herr Journal!! It turns out that Nathan Hooks likes me, and... he KISSED me on the beach! In Hawaii, on the shores of the ocean, my first kiss! How romance-novel-ish. And I don't even know this dude! And Mr. B caught Matthew coming out of our room tonight after curfew... *That was awkward.* But the good news is... Matthew does NOT like Phebe in any way! He told me so. He begged me not to "let" her like him. He was very firm that he does not like her. It's good that she and Aaron are going out now anyway.

Chapter 12: Beach Gossip

"Well, it's official!" Phebe announced on Monday afternoon, as she joined Joanna, Lisa, and Nicole on the beach under the scorching sun. This time, Joanna was wearing SPF 45, because she still loved feeling the warmth of the sun's rays on her skin. Phebe had gone to a late breakfast with Pelin, Dana, and some others, and was just now joining her friends on the sand. "Violet Flite had sex with Troy Milbourne last night at the luau. On the beach."

"What!" Lisa exclaimed in shock. As far as anyone knew, the school's one and only baton girl and Troy the trumpet player were not seeing each other.

Joanna groaned and rolled onto her stomach. Then she turned her head sideways as she straightened out the corner of her pink and white striped beach towel and said, "Really? How do you even know this?"

"I was just at breakfast with everyone!" Phebe explained. "Ask your brother. He was there. At breakfast, I mean. Not... when they were... you know..."

"And she just announced this to everyone?" Joanna challenged.

Phebe sighed, annoyed at the demand for these unimportant details. "No, *she* didn't. But all the guys were talking about it. Aaron told me, because Troy was bragging about it to all the guys. But I already knew because when Violet got up to go to the buffet, Pelin told all of us."

"Are they going out?" Lisa asked curiously.

Phebe shrugged. "I don't know. I guess there's some contest now with all the guys to see who all can get laid here in Hawaii."

"I'm going to throw up," Joanna said.

Nicole, who was lying next to her, said, "Me too."

"You know how we all made those rope-y twine flower bracelet thingeys at the luau?" Phebe went on. "Watch when you see the guys now. They're supposed to wear it on their right wrist, and then once they get laid here in Hawaii, they switch it to their left wrist." Phebe loved gossip. And just to be clear, in case anyone didn't follow the explanation of the bracelet protocol, she added, "So Troy has his on his left wrist now. And he's like, the hero of all the guys."

"Does Mr. B know about this?" Joanna asked incredulously.

"Of course not!"

Joanna found all of this to be totally disgusting. It was so far off from her moral compass that she didn't even know what to say. It disgusted her that all of her high school peers could be so flippant about something she considered to be sacred and private. She muttered to Phebe, "So, then, are you gonna go do it with Aaron now? So he can join the Lay Club and be a 'hero'?"

"No way!" Phebe cried, as if this was the most ridiculous idea ever. "We're not even going out!"

Lisa piped in with, "Well, evidently you don't have to be! Look at Violet and Troy!" while Nicole asked, "Wait, you're *not* going out? I thought you guys were going out now!"

Phebe shook her head. "We're buds. I mean, yeah, I guess we're 'going out,' but we're not like *going out-out*," she said, as if this clarified everything. "We're like, Joanna-and-Nathan going out, not like Christopher-and-Nicole going out."

"Oh," Nicole smiled. "So you're not in love yet. You're just seeing if you like each other enough."

"Yeah, sure."

"Where is Nathan today, anyway?" Lisa asked Joanna, hoping that Joanna still wasn't feeling like she wanted to throw up.

"I don't know," Joanna said into her towel. Her face was buried in it again as she lay on her stomach with her arms folded up under her forehead. "He's supposed to come find me later to go to lunch."

"Nathan wants to go on that Party Cruise," Phebe told them then. There was a hint of arrogance in her tone, simmering with satisfaction that she once again had the headlines.

Joanna popped her head up and looked straight forward, at the level of the sidewalk where the sand blended into the walkway in front of the hotels. Of course Phebe would have more current information on Joanna's beau than Joanna would. "Shut up."

"I think it sounds fun, Jay," Phebe said. "I think we should all go on it. It's gotta be safe, if all these people are promoting it. They must have a system to keep everything safe."

"I'm not going on a party cruise," Lisa said, knowing that Joanna would appreciate the support. "I can't afford it. It's like a hundred bucks!"

"A hundred bucks!" Joanna cried. "I'm not paying –"

"I'm not either," Nicole said. "Christopher joked that it sounded cool but even he didn't think it could really be safe."

"Well, I'm just saying, they were talking at breakfast about doing it tonight, and Nathan said he wants to do it."

***

Joanna's sunburn, which had gotten worse, was at its peak on Tuesday during their performance at Pearl Harbor, and after the show, she was near tears from the pain. Evidently an entire bottle of pure aloe wasn't enough to soothe her skin. Each time she raised her arms with the heavy poms, the skin on her shoulders felt like it was on fire. She was sure it would crack and break apart right then and there. She was wearing a strapless bra, but the underwires in it were cutting through the tender red skin on her chest.

"What's the matter, Jay?" Matthew asked her as they all walked back to the bus. "You don't look so good."

"Her bra is hurting her sunburn," Lisa explained. Matthew was the only guy, besides Christopher, that the girls would mention undergarments to.

"You should take it off if it hurts that bad," Matthew suggested.

Joanna smiled. On paper such a suggestion would look piggish, but coming from Matthew, the girls knew it was merely a suggestion of practicality. Joanna couldn't even imagine, however, reaching her arms around to unfasten the strap. She cringed at the thought of crinkling up her skin like that.

"Want me to unhook it for you?" Matthew asked politely, again, not being piggish, but just trying to be helpful. He winked at Joanna. "I'm good at this. I can do it one-handed! It comes from those old seventh and eighth grade pranks, you know."

Joanna giggled again. She remembered in middle school when Matthew and Christopher were practicing un-doing a bra one-handed, that they had strapped around a large teddy bear. They claimed that they never intended to actually use this skill on a real girl, but they loved the idea of being able to do it, "just in case."

Matthew reached behind Joanna and unsnapped her bra with one hand in a matter of a half-second. It dropped to the bottom of her performance t-shirt, which was tucked into the waistline of her pom skirt.

Joanna closed her eyes with relief and smiled. She looked at Matthew and said, "Okay, I can't believe I just let you do that, but THANK YOU!!!"

"Great, Matthew," Lisa applauded him. "Now, since you're so into being a gentleman, why don't you carry her bag for her so that the strap isn't wearing away on her shoulder! And Joanna, hold your poms up now in front of your chest so that you don't look all nippily."

They walked along the path a little farther, and Nathan came up to join them. "You okay, Joanna?" he asked. "Here, I can carry your bag for you." He took the bag from Matthew.

"Yeah, my sunburn just really hurts," she replied.

"Oh no..." Nathan sighed compassionately. "I thought you were wearing, like, SPF ninety-five or something!"

"Yeah, *now* I am. But it's too late for the critical places."

Nathan tried to talk to Joanna more on the bus, but she was pretty quiet. Nathan was so nice, and funny, and he seemed *really* into her, but she wasn't quite sure yet what she thought about this whole thing.

The bus made a stop at a nature preserve where everyone could walk around and take pictures, and then they headed back to the hotel on Waikiki Beach. Again, Nathan hung onto Joanna and showered her with attention, but she did not feel well and was not very responsive. Lisa sat with her on the bus on the way home.

When everyone was back at the hotel, Matthew came up to Joanna, put his arm around her carefully so as not to irritate her sunburn, and led her out the back way to the garden area near a walking path. "So, Jay, talk to me," he said. "What's up with Nathan?"

"I don't know!" Joanna cried. She sat on a low rock wall under a palm tree. She pulled a tube of lip balm out of her bag and swiped it across her lips. "I guess I kind of ignored him today. I feel bad, but –"

"I guess you *kind of* ignored him!" Matthew cried at the understatement. "Holy cow!"

Joanna sighed. "Matthew, I do not feel well today at all. My sunburn hurts so bad, I'm tired, and... Well, to be perfectly honest, I don't think it's a good idea for him and me to be 'going out' or whatever."

"Why not?" Matthew asked gently.

Joanna paused, and then she admitted what was really the problem now. "I heard about the little bet all you guys have going on, about who can get laid on the trip. I just don't want Nathan to think..."

"Ahhhhh," Matthew said. "I get it. I get it now. Oh Jay. That was just a dumb joke at breakfast the other day. Nobody's really going around trying to score. Well, except the real pigs, like Troy."

"Well, I don't know Nathan very well!" Joanna defended her concerns. "He's in the popular group! They're all players, aren't they? Is he going to expect to get some major action if we're going out? Because I'm not that kind of girl."

Matthew chuckled and rubbed her arm. "Ohhh, Jay. He knows you're not that kind of girl. He really likes you. And he's super confused right now because he thought you liked him too, but today you hardly talked to him at all!"

Joanna thought for a moment, and then said, "Well, what about the bracelet thing? That really bothers me." She looked down at Matthew's wrists and noticed he was not wearing a bracelet on either one of them.

Matthew just shook his head. "Yeah, I know. It bothers me too. It's not right, but there are pigs out there, and Violet... Yeah, it's not really that surprising, is it? Let's be honest. There are a few in this group that are on a different moral plane than the rest of us. It's going to be that way anywhere you go Jay, and we'll see it more as we get older. But Nathan knows you're not like that, and he is drawn to you for that."

Joanna smiled again. She loved sitting with Matthew – He was such a good friend. She felt safe with him, and she wished she could feel this safe with other guys she knew.

***

That night, the girls were too tired and sunburned to do anything, so they just hung around their hotel suite with the balcony doors open. They got popcorn and snacks from the ABC store, and left their door slightly ajar for anyone who wanted to stop by.

"I wonder if this is what college dorm life is like," Lisa pondered.

"I hope so," Phebe said, as she shook a bottle of nail polish. "This is fun. Even though I'd rather be going to the strip club tonight."

"Are they really going?" Joanna challenged, as she sat in the big cushy arm chair and grabbed the telephone. She thought of all the buzz about going on the Party Cruise the other night, and nobody ended up going.

"How come you're not going with them?" Nicole asked Phebe. Nicole was prepping for her date with Christopher.

Phebe shrugged. "I guess I'm kind of afraid of getting in trouble!" she laughed, and Joanna rolled her eyes. Phebe was such a talker, but usually she came to her senses. Joanna loved that about her.

"Well, good!" Nicole nodded approvingly. "You made the right choice. Have fun tonight, gals!" She headed out the door, leaving a trail of her fancy perfume behind her.

Joanna called her family while Phebe re-painted Joanna's toenails. She talked to her parents first, but then her sister Jodie got on the line.

Joanna and Jodie weren't always close, but they seemed to bond more when they were away from each other. Now that Jodie was in high school also, and now that Jodie seemed to be maturing at a rate that met her older sister's approval, the bond between them had grown.

Joanna had a lot of updates for her sister. It started with Phebe yelling in the background, "Joanna's got a boyfriend, Jodes!"

"Well, kind of, I think," Joanna explained into the phone, as Phebe blew on her toes to speed up the drying of the first coat of polish. "Do you know who Nathan Hooks is?" Then she went on to tell her about the luau, the kiss, and the Party Cruise. "By the way," she added, "this is all privileged sister-info, and is not to be shared with Mom or Dad or any brothers."

Jodie giggled and promised to keep quiet. "Can I tell Mom about your boyfriend?"

"Well, let's just wait and see if it even lasts through this trip," Joanna said wisely. "I'll introduce him when we get home if he's still worth introducing."

I don't even know what I think about life these days, Herr Journal. So many people are pigs. Sometimes Phebe scares me; I'm afraid she's being pulled down the wrong path. Thank goodness I have Lisa still being boring and safe with me. I like Nathan... Matthew assured me he's safe. I want to get to know Nathan better. I think I really do like him!

But then there's Matthew. I have such a strong *Freundschaft* with him, and I love talking to him. He's so caring and kind. He doesn't like Phebe, so that is a HUGE relief! Pelin and Dana are at a strip club tonight. They are such losers. I'm rambling now. I wish Mom were here... She'd help me sort some of this out.

Chapter 13: Antics

Joanna gave things with Nathan another chance the next day. Her sunburn felt better, and they spent time together snorkeling and exploring the beautiful landscapes on the group's excursion. She let him kiss her again, this time near a waterfall. It was a tender kiss, and this time she didn't stop it as quickly.

Joanna decided she liked kissing. It was fun, and she loved the way Nathan's tongue danced around in her mouth. It caused a surge of elation that she'd never experienced before, and she relaxed enough now to enjoy it. She carried her lip balm with her everywhere. There weren't too many occasions when they were totally alone, but they did get in some private moments by the waterfalls. He held her hand as they walked along the trails, and he made her a flower necklace at the Hula Hut near the shore. He pinched her butt when the whole group was walking out to the beach area, and he gave her a peck on the cheek as he helped her fasten her goggles on with her snorkel gear.

At one point late in the afternoon, when everyone was waiting for their bus and eating a snack, Christopher came over and sat down next to his sister. "You bein' a good girl?" he asked her. "Mickels said you guys have been makin' out all day."

Joanna rolled her eyes. "That's not true, Christopher. We have *not* been *making out* all day. And why is Aaron Mickels so interested in what Nathan and I are doing anyway? I thought he was trying to get it on with Phebe."

Christopher just shook his head and stood up again. "Well, just behave yourself, Jo-Jo. Don't give those jokers anything to talk about."

He started to walk away and Joanna called after him, "Well, tell those jokers to mind their own business and stop lookin' for gossip!" She smiled to herself. She hoped that she and Nathan could go for a nice long romantic walk along the beach later that night. She'd love it if he would hold her hand the whole way!

A small group that included the boys from the 30th floor went for a walk along the beach that night with Joanna, Phebe, Nicole, and Lisa. Nathan did hold Joanna's hand, and she decided this was okay, even if they weren't alone. They went into an ABC store, kidded about the "two-sixty-nines," and Nathan tried to buy some wine coolers. Joanna, the rule-follower, was relieved that the clerk carded him, and he was stuck just buying Pepsi and popcorn instead.

"Aren't you embarrassed that the worker caught you?" Joanna asked him when they got back outside. "You're lucky they didn't call the manager and have you arrested!"

"Nah," Nathan scoffed. "I'm sure kids do that all the time. It works sometimes, so it was worth a try."

"I would have been mortified," Joanna told him.

"Well, you wouldn't have even tried it," Lisa pointed out.

"That's true."

The guys invited everyone to come up to their room to play cards, but as they were getting off the elevator on the 30th floor, Mr. B came down the hallway. "Nathan," he said sternly, with a look that implied a deeper meaning than his voice indicated. "The ladies are not to be in there."

Joanna, Lisa, Phebe, and Nicole all slowly turned around and stepped back into the elevator, which luckily, hadn't closed yet.

"Boy, do I ever feel cheap," Nicole grumbled once the doors shut.

"Why is Mr. B such a dick?" Phebe wondered angrily.

Joanna was not quick to criticize the authority of their chaperone, as she felt some comfort in his enforcement of the rules. But she remembered the other night, when Mr. B saw Matthew leaving her room, when his sternness toward Matthew made her feel cheap. Perhaps Mr. B was going a *little* bit overboard.

"So much for playing cards," Lisa said sadly.

"And my kiss good-night!" Nicole whined.

Joanna looked up as the doors opened on the 28th floor. "And my popcorn!" she cried. "Nathan has my popcorn in the bag with his Pepsi!"

***

While Joanna's group had been innocently hanging out on the beach that night, Pelin, Dana, Violet, Troy, and some others ended up getting fake IDs and drinking all night at a nearby night club. At breakfast the next morning, word had spread like wildfire, but everyone kept quiet about it with the chaperones.

"So, is that why she's wearing her sunglasses, even though we're sitting under the shelter in the shade?" Joanna mocked with a hint of satisfaction to Christopher, confirming once again that she did not like Pelin. And although she felt sad that pom season would be over after this trip, she certainly wouldn't miss dealing with Pelin Yilmaz and Dana Strohbeck anymore.

"Yeah, she's hurtin' today!" Christopher laughed. "Poor little thing."

"Yeah, poor little drunk. What a loser." Only with her brother would Joanna whisper such unkind words.

There was a performance that afternoon, but Violet Flite sat off to the side, crying, and not participating. She wasn't even wearing her sparkly leotard; she was wearing jean shorts and a light cotton, short-sleeved, zipper hoodie. There was no mention of the baton girl, and the band played while the pom squad performed as if they always performed without a baton girl. The only difference was that the band did not play their isolated baton feature piece that usually followed one of the pom routines.

When Joanna saw Violet crying during the performance, she began to feel sorry for her, unable to imagine what the smooth, confident Violet Flite could be so upset about.

"Why isn't Violet performing today?" Joanna asked Matthew during the Trumpet Feature, when the percussionists and pom girls were on a short break. "She's crying over there. Shouldn't someone go see if she's okay?"

Matthew touched Joanna's arm and said, "She's okay, Jay. She's crying because she got in a boatload of trouble with Mr. B this morning and he won't let her perform."

Oooh! This could be good!

"What'd she get in trouble for?" Joanna asked, hoping her calm tone would mask the burning curiosity that fueled her interest now.

Matthew lowered his voice and leaned closer to Joanna. "She has a *huge* hickey on the back of her neck, and also one on the front of her collarbone. It's super obvious when she's wearing that dance thing to perform. Mr. B was fuming, but he contained himself when he just told us simply that we're not doing a baton feature today, and that we should just do everything else like normal except not the baton piece."

"Wow..." Joanna said, looking away in thought. She remembered some of the tricks in the dance world. "They couldn't cover it up with make-up? Or put a band-aid on it or anything?"

"Nope, he wouldn't even let her try. He was so mad! He called her parents and made her tell them why she wasn't going to be performing today. She's probably most embarrassed about that, and that he made her come to the performance anyway even though she can't do anything."

Good, Joanna decided firmly inside her head. *At least Mr. B is holding her accountable for her bad, shameful behavior.*

In the evening after their performance, the girls stayed out longer to go shopping on Waikiki Beach. Later, Phebe and Joanna found themselves completely in the dark when they returned to their hotel room and opened the door. Only a sliver of light from the moon and streetlights outside shone in through the windows and balcony door.

Phebe reached to flick on the switch for the overhead light in the kitchen, but it didn't work. The lamps in the living room and bedrooms were out too. "Joanna, call the front desk and tell them our power is out," Phebe instructed.

If the phone even works, Joanna wondered silently. She knew something was fishy because the refrigerator and the air conditioning were still working, but when she picked up the phone, there was indeed no dial tone. "The phone doesn't work," Joanna reported.

"Okay, now I'm scared," Phebe said.

"Scared?" Joanna scoffed. "I don't think we have to be *scared.* It probably just blew a fuse or something." Phebe could be dramatic at times.

The girls walked into the hallway and saw two other girls from band waiting for the elevator, so they asked them if they had power. Since they did, the girls let them use their phone to call the front desk.

After Joanna and Phebe returned to their dark room to wait, Nicole came home and asked why they were sitting in the dark.

"All the lights are out," Phebe explained. "We don't have power."

"The *lights*?" Nicole asked in disbelief. "*Just* the lights?"

Joanna went into their bedroom and noticed that the digital clock on the nightstand was still working. "Okay," she said. "Duh! Why is the clock working and not the lamp, when they are plugged into the same outlet?"

"Oh. My. Lord!" Nicole cried, as she reached under the lamp shade and twisted the bulb. Suddenly the light came on. "You guys!" she laughed. "They unscrewed all our lightbulbs!" She walked over to the other nightstand to screw in that bulb, and the room lit up.

The girls had a pretty good idea of who "they" were, as they scowled and ran around the rooms, re-screwing in all the lightbulbs. "Now we just have to figure out what the deal is with the phone," Phebe said. "I bet they took the cord!"

"Those turds!" Joanna cried. "C'mon!" The three girls ran to the stairwell and darted up to the 30th floor. They didn't have time to wait for that slow elevator; they pounded on the door to suite 3002.

Matthew answered, but he only peeked his head out. "Go away!" he whispered desperately. "Seriously! We unscrewed all your lightbulbs. Your underwear is in the couch and in the stove. Please don't tell! Please! Now go! Before we get in more trouble!"

Our underwear???

Joanna had never seen such desperation in Matthew's face. As Phebe and Nicole ran to the stairwell to head back down to their floor, Joanna said, "Okay, but where's our phone cord?"

"I don't know!" Matthew pleaded, still whispering. "Aaron did that. It's under the TV, I think. *Please* don't tell!" He shut the door.

The girls ran back down to their room, and Phebe was already crying. "*Our underwear* is in the couch!" When they got into the room, Nicole pulled the phone cord out from underneath the TV stand and plugged it back in. "I got my period yesterday!" Phebe panicked, as she lifted one of the couch cushions. "If they found anything from that..."

Under one cushion was a pile of Nicole's 'delicates,' all clean, all very lacy and pretty. Under another cushion was a pile of Joanna's own pretty bras and underwear, and to her relief, all clean as well. Inside the stove was a heap of plain, regular underwear, which they assumed must have been Lisa's since they weren't Phebe's. Phebe was relieved that none of hers had been touched.

Once she got the phone cord plugged back in, Joanna called up to the boys' room. Colvin answered, and said that Nathan couldn't come to the phone. In fact, nobody could come to the phone. "I'll come down there," Colvin told her. "I'd better just come down there and talk to you guys."

A few minutes later, Colvin came down to the girls' room and used some colorful words to describe the type of trouble that the other boys were in. The conclusion was that Matthew, Christopher, Nathan, and Aaron were confined to their room. "Yeah, the other night they all went into Pelin and Dana's room and moved all their furniture onto the balcony, and moved all the balcony furniture inside," he explained.

Joanna smiled and rolled her eyes, Nicole laughed, and Phebe muttered something about them all being a bunch of dumbheads. A knock came to the door then, and Joanna, remembering the night before, whispered to Colvin, "You'd better hide, Jaynort. It's probably Mr. B."

Colvin refused to hide. He sat comfortably on the couch while Joanna answered the door.

It was Mr. B. "Mr. Jaynort, I thought I made myself clear about being in other people's rooms," he said sternly. "Now go, before I really get mad."

Colvin left with his head bowed and without saying a word.

"Now, ladies," Mr. B continued. "What's this about you not having power?"

"Oh, that's not a problem anymore. Sir." Phebe spoke confidently, with wide, innocent eyes. "The lights were out when we got home, but then all of a sudden, they just came back on. We're not sure what happened. But it's fine now."

"Um-hmm," Mr. B nodded, but he did not appear as though he believed one word of what Phebe had just said. "Okay. And also, you are not to call 3002. And you are not to be up there, either. They are grounded."

"Yes, Sir."

Mr. B left.

Chapter 14: Values

When Joanna and Nicole got into their beds that night, they chatted for a few minutes like they usually did, but then Nicole became serious.

"Joanna, can I ask you a question?" she said quietly, in the darkness. The air conditioning was running, and the bedroom door was closed, so there were no worries about anyone hearing their conversation.

"Sure," Joanna replied, now curious.

Nicole took a deep breath. "What do you think about premarital sex?"

Joanna's eyes widened, although no one would have known that in the dark. She was quiet for a moment, while her mind scurried for thoughts on how to respond. She realized Nicole must be contemplating having sex with Christopher!

"Well..." Joanna began carefully. Christopher and Nicole had been dating since the previous summer. They seemed to be a very stable, strong couple, and Nicole got along beautifully with everyone in their group. It made sense that at this point, the topic of advancing their physical relationship would be on their minds.

But premarital sex was definitely a no-no in the Conors Family Value System! Joanna and her siblings had been raised to regard sex as the highest, most sacred of all forms of intimacy between a man and a woman, and that level of intimacy was to be experienced *only* within the context of a marriage. More so than it being too big of a risk of getting pregnant or a disease, sex outside of a marriage was simply *wrong*.

Nicole was a 'good girl,' but Joanna had to consider that Nicole felt truly in love with Christopher. She realized then that it was easy to hold onto these values when the opportunity to compromise them wasn't there.

Joanna chose her words carefully. "Um... Well, we were raised in our family that sex is something that should only be experienced within a marriage." Nicole was quiet, so Joanna decided to cut to the chase. "Are you and Christopher thinking about having sex?"

Joanna didn't like to think about this idea. In fact, it sort of made her feel sad, as well as sick to her stomach. She loved her brother, and he was her hero. She didn't want him to do anything 'wrong,' or anything he would regret. But at the same time, they were both growing up now, and there were going to be times when they would face some big decisions.

"We've been talking about it," Nicole admitted. "It just seems like such a great opportunity, to be here together in *Hawaii*, and it would be just so perfect, if we're going to do it, to do it here."

Joanna half-smiled in the darkness and said, "Yeah... I can see where that idea would be appealing." She thought about Nathan kissing her for the first time on the rocks near the calming ocean waves.

"But would it be wrong?" Nicole asked her. "I mean, we love each other, and we are in love with each other, right?"

"Well, I guess it depends on how you guys both view it," Joanna offered. "I mean, for me, personally, for *me*, I want to be a virgin for my husband. I want my *husband* to be the absolute only person on the planet that I will ever share my body with. I don't want to have a history when I find the man that I will marry someday. I know Christopher has always said that too; he is saving himself for marriage, and he won't want a girl that's slept with anyone else. He won't want a wife that's been with other guys before him, because that is the one thing that should be so sacred between a husband and wife. It's just how we were raised."

"I know," Nicole whispered softly. "I was raised that way too."

"You know, we're only eighteen, Nicole," Joanna pointed out, as she thought about how her mother might respond to this dilemma. "It seems old because we're the oldest on this trip, we're the oldest at school, we'll be *graduating* in two and a half months, but really, there's a whole lifetime ahead of us after 'tomorrow.' We've still got a lot of years before we'll be ready for marriage. A lot can happen in that time."

"Yeah, that's my big worry," Nicole said. "I'm afraid... Well, first of all, I'm terrified of getting pregnant, so obviously we'd use a *two-sixty-nine*, but outside of that, I still worry that we might not be together forever. Although right now that doesn't seem possible because we are so in love!"

"Well, I guess what you have to think about then, is what are you willing to live with? If you guys do it here, and then you end up breaking up, are you okay with having given your virginity to someone that you're no longer with, but still know that it was very romantic being in Hawaii? Would you be okay with not being a virgin for the next guy that comes along?" Joanna didn't want to draw attention to the alternative side of this decision, such as, how would Nicole feel if she *didn't* do it here. Would she regret not taking the romantic opportunity? Joanna desperately did not want her brother and Nicole to have sex yet, but she wanted to be fair to her friend, whose circumstances were quite different than what Joanna had ever experienced herself yet.

Nicole was quiet, so Joanna concluded with, "Well, Nicole, it's easy for me to lay here and preach that you shouldn't have sex no matter what until you're married. But I don't know what it's like to be truly in love with someone so much so that I would be willing to give him my everything. I guess you have to think about what's more important to you: the romance of giving your virginity to your current boyfriend on the shores of the Pacific Ocean? Or saving yourself, knowing that having premarital sex is wrong no matter what the circumstances are."

Nicole was quiet in thought again for a few moments, and then she said, "You are so wise, Joanna."

Joanna smiled proudly and said, "Well, I have two very smart parents who aren't afraid to talk about these things with us."

***

It was pretty quiet at breakfast the next morning. The boys were not allowed to talk or sit with anyone else in the whole band or pom group; they were given to-go boxes to get their food and return to their room. Violet had to sit in isolation.

"Why isn't Troy Milbourne being punished?" Joanna asked Pelin, who was sitting near her.

Pelin swallowed a chunk of breakfast potatoes and just looked at Joanna. "Why would Troy be punished?" she said. Her tone was borderline snarky, and immediately Joanna realized this was not the time for this conversation. Pelin could be very unpredictable.

Joanna maintained her assertiveness. Being this assertive with someone like Pelin was a bit out of her comfort zone, but she wanted answers! "Well, isn't he the one who gave Violet all those hickeys?"

Pelin shrugged and pushed some food around on her plate with her fork. "Nobody," she said coolly, "including Violet, will tell Mr. B who gave her

After Tomorrow

the hickeys, so he can't punish anyone for that. Besides, even if someone did rat on Troy, he'd just deny it, and Mr. B can't prove it." She got up and walked away.

Joanna was flabbergasted at the knavery surrounding her.

Nicole came back to the table with her plate of eggs, fuming. "I am so pissed!" she exploded when she sat down. "They just told me that Mr. B actually went to the *airport* early this morning to try to get return tickets for all those guys! He's going to send them all home!"

"What?!" Joanna and Lisa dropped their forks.

Now Joanna was fired up. She thought about her brother, and Matthew. And Nathan! She couldn't imagine finishing out the rest of this trip without them! "That is insane!" she exclaimed in a loud whisper. "How can he send home half the drumline and all his trumpets, just for a silly little prank, when Pelin and Dana and all those other sluts are out getting fake IDs and drinking and bringing guys into their rooms!" Joanna didn't really know if that last part was true – she hadn't heard anything about bringing guys into rooms – but she decided in her fury that it was probably true.

Nicole piped in, "I swear if he sends them home, I'm ratting on all the girls who were..."

"Nobody's being sent home," Phebe announced, joining them at the table. She climbed into the bench to sit next to Joanna, and she set down her orange juice. "The only tickets he could get on short notice would be going through Seattle, and they were like seven hundred dollars apiece, or something, and Mr. B didn't want to make their parents pay all that money."

"It was probably just a big scare then," Lisa suggested, as Joanna and Nicole breathed sighs of relief.

"Well, they're still grounded, though," Phebe went on, pleased that once again, she was the one with the latest headlines. "We're performing today without the drumline because Matthew's the main percussionist, and his only backup is grounded too, and we'll be down a few trumpets and Nathan's trombone. And they'll all miss the excursion afterwards when we go to see the sea turtles."

"This is so dumb," Joanna complained. "I'm calling my parents tonight."

Herr Journal, this is so insane! Pelin and Dana and some others are out drinking, fake ID-ing, and strip-clubbing here in Hawaii, and getting away with it. Meanwhile, Christopher and Matthew and Nathan and some of the guys played one innocent little prank, which we didn't even care about! And Mr. B suspended them from performing and was even going to SEND THEM HOME!!! I called Dad tonight, and he and Matthew's dad raised holy hell with Mr. B about going overboard with the punishments. So I guess the guys will be back with us for our last day tomorrow. But still. Ugh!

After Tomorrow

Chapter 15: Boyfriend

With only one full day left of the trip, everyone wanted to soak up as much sun as they could. The group spent the afternoon up on the rooftop of the hotel, throwing each other in and out of the pool. The pool water was so cold that it made the ocean water seem warm, but the hot tub made up for that.

At one point, Joanna and Nathan were the only two in the hot tub, and they held hands under the surface of the bubbling water. The others in the main pool would yell things to them like, "Hey! Hand check!" or "Hey! Keep it *G* over there!" Joanna had relaxed on the idea of having a 'boyfriend,' and she was really starting to like Nathan. He kissed her a few times when they hoped no one else was paying attention to what was going on in the hot tub, but later Phebe told her that she saw them kiss. Joanna didn't care, knowing they had remained respectable.

"So, are we, like, going out? Or what?" Joanna asked Nathan late that last evening. The two of them were walking along the beach, just like she had been waiting for, and he was holding her hand.

"Yeah!" he replied enthusiastically. "Yeah, I think we are! I mean, I'd like us to be going out. I'd like you to be my girlfriend."

Joanna smiled. "Okay, Nathan. I'm your girlfriend then. But... well, I've never really had a real boyfriend before," she admitted. "So..."

"Well, *that* I can't believe!" he said. Nathan was charming. "I noticed you long ago, but I was sure you were taken."

Joanna thought that sounded kind of silly. Everyone knew everyone in Woodland Hills, and if someone at Liberty High School had a boyfriend, everyone at Liberty High School knew it.

"I figured you had some fancy rich boyfriend that was hand-picked from up in Edina or something," Nathan went on, referencing an elite suburb of the Twin Cities.

Joanna's intuition told her that this was all a bunch of schmoozing, but since she liked Nathan and was excited that he liked her, she said, "Well, what should I tell my parents? I mean, do I just say, *Hey, I'd like you to meet my boyfriend, Nathan?"*

"Sure, I guess!"

When they got back to the hotel, Phebe and Lisa met them outside by the construction mess of the front entrance. "You missed it, Jay. We went to *Jackoff-of-all-Trades* one last time."

Joanna, still holding Nathan's hand, looked at her *boyfriend.* "That's okay," she said. "My belly would have exploded if I'd eaten a butter burger this late at night."

Phebe looked up at the tower of the Palm Residences hotel and sighed. "Our last night in our crap-site," she mused wistfully. "I'm going to miss our little crap-site!"

Joanna giggled and Phebe and Lisa took off.

Instead of going into the open lobby then, Nathan led Joanna behind a palm tree where all the construction rubble was, and he gently kissed her on the lips again. She savored the dance of his tongue, realizing that it might be a while before they would be alone again. And it would be a *really* long time before she'd be in a beautiful tropical place like Hawaii again, toying with romance.

"Good night, Joanna," Nathan finally said, looking into her eyes under the moonlight. He brushed a wisp of her hair behind her ear. "Thanks for going out with me and for making this trip so fun."

Joanna stood on her tiptoes and kissed her *boyfriend* quickly on the cheek. "This trip was fun!" she agreed. "Good night, Nathan."

When Joanna got up to her suite, she waltzed through the door with a starry gaze in her eyes. "Hel-looo," she sang happily.

"Oh brother, *that* is the look of a girl in love," Phebe said. "Here's your popcorn, by the way, from the other night." She tossed a bag of popcorn from the ABC store across the room to her friend.

Joanna plopped down on the arm chair and opened her snack.

"Did you make out all night or what?" Phebe asked dryly.

Joanna looked over at her with a hint of mystery in her eyes. "We had a very nice evening together, if you must know," she said.

"And??"

"And... The rest is between me and Nathan."

Phebe rolled her eyes and changed the subject to her dilemma of not being able to fit the three new pairs of shoes she'd purchased on the trip into her suitcase.

***

As they lay in their beds that night, Nicole said quietly to Joanna, "Well, Joanna, I just want you to know that Christopher and I decided we're *not* going to have sex while we're here in Hawaii."

Joanna kept her sigh of relief silent. "You did, huh? Well, that's probably smart," she said.

"It's just not the right time," Nicole went on. "It's definitely on our minds, but I really want to wait until I'm married for this."

"I think that is smart," Joanna repeated. "But it's good that you guys talk about it, so that you're on the same page!"

"Yes, we both agreed that we need to be on the same page. Thanks for letting me talk through this with you, Joanna. You really gave me some good advice. And I know I can trust you, that you're not going to share our conversation with anyone else."

"Of course," Joanna confirmed. "Anytime, Nicole. I'm a safe confidante."

***

Joanna and Nathan sat together on the plane for the long flights home the next day, and they held hands much of the time. They talked and joked with their friends around them, but they also talked privately with each other.

"What's that book you're writing in?" he asked her when she pulled out her journal and a pen. "Is it your diary?"

"Yep! I named it *Herr Journal*," she told him.

Nathan looked confused. "So... this is a *hair* journal?"

"No!" Joanna giggled.

Nathan pretended to scribble onto the page of an invisible book. "*Oh, today I pulled it all up on top of my head like this...*"

Joanna giggled again. "*Herr* is *Mister* in German."

"Mr. Journal," Nathan repeated. Then he teased in a high-pitched voice, *"Dear Mr. Hair Journal. Ugh. I was so frustrated today. My hair was so flat, and it wouldn't hold the curls. It was such a bad hair day!"*

"Yeah, ha ha. For your information, Mr. Nathan Hooks, I don't write about my hair. I write about all of my *Freundschafts.*"

"Freundschafts? Is that more German?"

"Yep! *Freundschaft* means *friendship* in German."

"Can I read this book?"

"No way!" Joanna exclaimed, closing the book and tossing it back into her little bag.

"You gonna write about *my* hair in there?" he joked with his big, captivating smile. Joanna found his smile – with that one tooth slightly in front of the other – to be so sexy!

Joanna smiled – with her perfect white teeth and creases at the sides of her lips – and shrugged mysteriously. "Maybe."

Nathan squeezed her hand again and sighed happily. "I can't wait to go back to school on Monday and show off my new *girlfriend.*"

Joanna thought about that for a moment. This was going to be a little weird. She had never had a 'boyfriend' – officially – before. And usually when there was an officially-dating couple at school, the whole student body got into their business.

And she still wasn't sure about her parents.

The plane landed in Minneapolis, and then there was the long bus ride back to Liberty High School in Woodland Hills. It was balmy for a March evening – upper 30's! – and the families were waiting outside in the school parking lot when the bus pulled in. Joanna ran up and hugged her parents. Jodie and Nick were there also. Mrs. Conors handed Joanna her pink pompom hat.

"You are so tan!" Jodie cried enviously as she hugged her sister. Joanna's skin radiated from its exposure to the tropics, though right now Jodie could only see her face.

Christopher was wearing a straw sunhat with real flowers woven around it, which seemed to shiver at the abrupt change in temperature. He took it off his head and set it on his little brother's head. "I got you a souvenir, Bud!"

After Tomorrow

"Aw, cool!" Nick marveled as he took the hat off his head to look at it.

Mr. Conors put his arm around his daughter and said, "I hear you've found yourself a boyfriend while you were off frolicking in the tropics."

Joanna shot a glance at her sister, and Jodie shrugged. "Um... Well, yeah," Joanna said. "He's over there. Come meet him!" She pulled her parents over to where Nathan and his parents were standing, and Joanna, beaming, said, "Nathan, this is my mom and my dad."

"Oh, you are an adorable thing!" Nathan's mother exclaimed, coming up to Joanna and taking her hands into her own. The parents exchanged hellos, chatted for a few minutes, and then everyone headed home.

"Do you guys already know Nathan's parents?" Joanna asked her mom and dad curiously in the car as they drove out of the school parking lot.

"They own *the Lure*," Mr. Conors explained, referring to a small hole-in-the-wall bar in the north end of Woodland Hills. As a loan officer at the bank, he was familiar with the connections of families and small businesses in the community.

Christopher, who was squished next to Joanna in the middle row of the family's small SUV, looked over at her and rubbed his fingers and thumb together. He whispered, almost inaudibly, "They've got money."

I'm home, Herr Journal. Hawaii is behind us now, and it's back to reality in Woodland Hills. It's only about 40° here... that ought to give my sunburn a chance to heal. Ha ha, I'm so beautiful these days, you know, with all my skin peeling off my nose and cheeks. Nathan says it's cute and adorable. ☺ Dad doesn't seem too bothered about me having a boyfriend, and Nathan's parents are SUPER nice. I guess this might be okay!

Chapter 16: Par-tay!

News spread quickly at school on Monday, when everyone returned from Spring Break. Nathan Hooks and Joanna Conors were an 'item,' and right away they were invited to parties and other social engagements for the following weekend. Things remained somewhat casual, though. Sometimes Nathan would sit with Joanna's crew at lunch, and sometimes she'd go over to his usual table and sit with him and his popular friends. Udo Meikler and Dustin Rollick were buddies at Nathan's table, and one day they started talking up what they hoped would be a big bash on Saturday night.

"JC, everyone's getting together at Rollick's house on Saturday," Udo told her. "We're playing cards. You gonna come?"

Dustin turned to Nathan and said quietly, "You're bringing the juice, right?"

Nathan nodded confidently. "Yeah, I'll see what I can round up."

Joanna was only realizing now that since Nathan's parents owned a local bar, Nathan had ample access to liquor. This bumped him up to first place on the guest list when his classmates had parties.

***

Word about Joanna having a boyfriend also got out at the Toy Store. On Tuesday night when Joanna walked into the breakroom to hang up her jacket at the start of her shift, Ken, the manager, exclaimed, "How on earth did you get that dark, skiing in Colorado?"

Christopher was right behind her, along with Matthew. Mike Grenzesky and Luke Mason were back there as well, on their mid-shift break.

"Skiing in Colorado!" Joanna exclaimed, pushing up her sleeve and looking at her dark tanned arm, which was peeling. "That was Jill, Ken. Jill was in Colorado for Spring Break. We were in Hawaii."

"How were the islands?" Mike asked kindly, staring at Joanna. She had tried to smooth out all the peeling skin from her nose and cheeks, but her face was still a blotchy mess of pink and brown patches. The sweet smell of aloe radiated from her, within the stale air of the breakroom.

"Hot, wonderful, and I'm peeling like crazy," she said happily.

"They have this stuff nowadays," Ken joked with her. "It's this lotion that actually blocks the harmful UV rays of the sun when you put it on your skin. It's called sunblock."

Matthew looked at Ken and said with a twinkle in his eye, "Jay found herself a boyfriend while she was in the tropics."

"Who?" Ken asked excitedly. "You?!"

Christopher laughed and patted his buddy on the shoulder, while Matthew said, "No, she's aimin' a little higher than me, Ken. Found herself a rich dude."

"Really!" Ken exclaimed. "Is that true, Joanna?"

Joanna smiled. "Maybe!" She grabbed her time card and headed up to the front of the store.

Later, while Joanna was making room for a case of *Hungry Hungry Hippos* in the board game aisle, Luke sauntered up to her. "Yo," he said.

She looked at him. She wasn't sure what he meant, so she just replied, "Yo."

"I thought you were goin' out with Mike?" he asked her curiously.

She looked at him again. "Going out with Mike? Mike Grenzesky? Why would you think that?"

Luke shrugged. "Mike said you were going out."

"With *Mike*?" she clarified, confused. "As in, *dating... him*?" This was almost the strangest thing she had ever heard in her entire life!

"Yeah, he said he gives you rides home, and you guys went out for pie..."

"Luke, I am *not* dating Mike Grenzesky, and I have absolutely no desire to date him. I'm sorry if he misunderstood my intentions when I accepted a ride home."

"But you have a boyfriend in Hawaii?"

Joanna giggled. "My boyfriend is not *in Hawaii*. He goes to my school, and we started dating during the trip."

"Mike is heartbroken," Luke said dramatically, shaking his head.

"Well, he'll get over it," Joanna assured him, as she pushed the last *Hungry*

Hungry Hippos game onto the shelf.

***

On Saturday morning, as Christopher and Joanna drove to work together, Joanna asked her brother, "Are you and Nicole going to Dustin Rollick's party tonight?"

"Rollick's having a party?" he said. Then, "Nah. We aren't privy to that elite group. You've surpassed me on the social ladder, Jo-Jo, now that you're in with Hooks."

Joanna didn't say anything, so after a moment, Christopher asked her, "Why? Are you going?"

"I don't know. Nathan wants me to. I was hoping we could just go out to a movie or something, just me and him. But he wants to go to that party."

"He's kind of a partier, Jo-Jo," Christopher advised. He knew of his sister's aversion to drinking, so he added, "There's probably going to be a lot of booze there. Nathan's probably supplying it." Christopher was so socially smart. Joanna appreciated that her brother could keep her in the loop when she was too naïve to follow what was going on sometimes.

"How does he get liquor from their bar without his parents knowing?" she wondered.

Christopher shrugged. "I don't know. Maybe they do know, and they don't care."

"His mom is so nice, though!"

"Well, Jo-Jo! Nice people drink too, you know!"

On Saturday afternoon, Nathan stopped by the Toy Store to see Joanna. "Hey," he said, when he came up to the Customer Service Area where she was handling refunds. "So, I was thinking of not going to that party tonight, and taking you to a movie instead."

Joanna's whole face lit up. "Really?"

Nathan smiled his fabulous smile, with that slightly crooked front tooth. She still found it sexy. "Yeah! *Soldier One* is out now; I think that one looks good."

Joanna beamed. She didn't care what the movie was, as long as they didn't have to go to the party. "This sounds great, Nathan!"

"Super! Can I pick you up here after work? We can go out to dinner and then hit the 9:00 show?"

"Yes! YAY!" Joanna was so relieved to be able to stay away from a drinking party that night that she could hardly think about anything else for the rest of her shift.

> The movie on our date tonight was fun, Herr Journal. And... we kissed. A LOT. I know what people mean now when they joke about not going to the movies for the movie! I am totally in love with Nathan, I think. He's hot, and he's fun. We're going out to lunch with Christopher and Nicole tomorrow. But I just want to kiss him and make out with him! Yikes! ☺

✳✳✳

Another week went by, and things were wonderful at school with Nathan. Joanna's official boyfriend now of a few weeks was sweet and attentive to her, and she was sweet and attentive to him. She looked forward to their next date, with the hope that they'd get some 'alone time' to kiss.

The *plan* for Saturday night was to just meet up with a bunch of friends at Riverside Billiards Hall, a popular weekend hangout for the locals. The billiards hall had a teen room with pool tables, dart boards, and the best stuffed-crust pizza in Woodland Hills. But the impulsive and unpredictable life of high school seniors, still experimenting with adult-like freedoms and responsible decision-making, put Joanna in a quandary on this particular evening.

Nathan pulled into the Conors' family driveway just before six o'clock. The engine of his dad's shiny new red Camaro roared to announce his arrival, ready to pick up Joanna and Christopher. Next stop was to pick up Phebe, then off to Riverside. Some people in the community bitterly referred to Nathan as a spoiled rich kid who, thanks to his parents' lucrative bar in the north end of town, would likely never have to work a day in his life. Others, however, viewed him as just a product of his environment: a nice young man who benefitted from his parents' affluence.

Many kids from school were at the pool hall, and things were going fine for a long time. But then as people started getting bored with darts and billiards, Pelin Yilmaz announced that her parents weren't home. Suddenly, everyone was heading over to her house.

"I guess we're all going over to Pelin's," Phebe shrugged casually to Joanna as the plans were being made. While a party like this was the norm for Pelin and the others in the popular group, it was all unchartered waters for Joanna and her crew. Now that Joanna was dating Nathan, Phebe and Lisa had an 'in' to the lives of those in the popular crowd.

Phebe was excited to be part of the elite group's party, but a pit started to form in Joanna's stomach. Her intuition was telling her that this wasn't a good idea. Pelin was wild, and Joanna knew there would be drinking if everyone was at her house without parental supervision.

Joanna looked around the hall and said distractedly, "Where's Christopher? Is he going?" She hated to admit it, but her brother was still her security blanket.

"What does it matter if he's going?" Phebe cried. "Nathan's going! He's our ride, so we have to go, Jay."

Nathan appeared from behind Joanna and put his arm around her. "Hey Babe! You ready to *par-tay* at Residence Yilmaz?"

"Her parents aren't home, Nathan," Joanna told him quietly.

"Joanna, you're being lame!" Phebe muttered. "We don't need a mommy and a daddy hovering over us every Saturday night."

"Well, I don't want Pelin to get in trouble!" Joanna justified defensively, even though that was a bold-faced lie. Joanna would love for Pelin to get in trouble, as long as Joanna was far away from it.

"Her parents don't care! She wouldn't have invited us all over if she was going to get in trouble."

"It's okay, Joanna," Nathan said calmly. He gently took her chin in his hand and turned her face to his. "It's fine. We're just going to go there and play cards and hang out, okay?"

Nathan's eyes appeared calm and safe, yet Joanna didn't trust the situation. She looked around the hall to find Christopher, so when her classmate Kaley Saint walked by, Joanna grabbed her arm. "Kaley," she said, "have you seen my brother?"

"Yeah, he was in the other room with Matthew and the other guys," she said. "You comin' to Pelin's?"

Desperate to find a way out of this, Joanna stammered, "Well, Christopher rode with me and Nathan, so…"

"Joanna, come on!" Phebe pulled her along as Nathan headed out the doors.

"It's okay, Joanna!" Kaley called after her. "Christopher can ride with us! We'll bring Lisa too!"

Nathan became a bit overconfident as he sped through the side streets of town to get to Pelin's house. When he parked the car, he said, "Hang on a sec, I have to get something out of the trunk." He retrieved a sturdy open box from the trunk; Joanna heard the clanging of glass bottles.

"Why'd you park so far away?" Phebe asked him accusingly as they trudged up the sidewalk for what seemed like forever. It was cold outside – the crisp late-March night air was bitter at this hour. They walked and walked, and soon they saw more cars near the house.

"I don't want anyone parking too close to my dad's Camaro," Nathan explained. "And I thought *that* was her house. But I guess it's that other red one up there."

A bunch of kids were already in the house when they walked in. As Nathan stepped inside, he held the box up over his head and yelled, "Who's ready to PAR-TAY?!!"

The sound of the clanging bottles shoved the lump in Joanna's stomach right up into her throat.

Things did not get better. Soon there were kids everywhere, mulling over the liquor in Nathan's box, appreciating his contribution to the party.

"This shit's ice cold!" Dustin Rollick jeered as he pulled out a bottle of tequila and quickly set it on the coffee table.

"Well, it was in my trunk!" Nathan laughed. "My mobile refrigeration system!"

"Alright, what else ya got, Pee-Pee?" Shana Saint, Kaley's identical twin sister, asked Pelin, who had opened up the liquor cabinet in their family room.

As Pelin read off the labels of the liquor bottles, Joanna turned to Phebe and whispered, "*Pee-Pee?*"

Phebe shrugged, hoping to convey a cool, relaxed manner in this environment where she, too, was a fish out of water. "That's what they all call her," she whispered back. Her eyes remained fixed on the scene, so as not to appear to be gossiping.

"Yeah, *they,* not *we,*" Joanna chided. Phebe was grasping at the next rung on that social ladder, and Joanna wasn't ready for it.

Kaley stepped up and put her arms around Joanna and Phebe. "This is so awesome!" she exclaimed. "There are a bunch of hot guys in the kitchen!" Pelin's twenty-one-year-old brother and several of his friends supplied a case of beer and some packs of cigarettes, and were now looking for some 'compensation' from the high school girls.

"Kaley, where's Christopher?" Joanna asked her, as someone turned on some music. Lisa was there now too, looking anxious.

"Oh," Kaley answered nonchalantly. "He and Matthew said they were going to stay at Riverside, and maybe go to Studio Six instead. He said Matthew will give him a ride home." She turned to go back into the kitchen, with Phebe at her heels.

Joanna watched nervously as everyone else opened beers and toyed with the alcohol. She plopped down on the couch, with uneasy thoughts scattering through her mind. *We are dead if the cops show up. My parents will kill me if I'm at an underage drinking party that gets busted by the cops! What is going to happen at this house?*

Nathan was the life of the party. Not only was he the hero for supplying most of the booze, but he knew how to drink it. "C'mon, Babe, do some shots with me!" he called over to Joanna from the coffee table.

Joanna tried to smile and replied, "I'm gonna sit this one out, Nathan."

"Aw, man, my girl don't like to drink!" he yelped playfully, as he tilted his head back with a shot of tequila. He was loud and jovial, commanding the attention of all around him.

Pelin's voice, confident and firm, rang from across the room, "*I'll* shoot these with you, Nate-dog." She treaded past Joanna, making a big show of stepping over Joanna's outstretched feet, and held out a shot glass to the bottle of Jose Cuervo. Nathan poured himself another shot, and the two downed the liquor in record time.

Suddenly Dana announced, "Uh-oh! First puke of the night!" as a girl threw up all over the kitchen floor. Then she cursed, yelling that the girl could have aimed for the trash.

Lisa came over to Joanna and sat next to her on the couch. "I'm not sure this is a good idea," she said softly. Her long brown hair was braided along the side of her head. She looked really pretty, even in all of her uncertainty.

"Ya think?" Joanna muttered disgustedly.

Phebe appeared from somewhere and said, "Here, Lisa, try this!" She held a small clear punch cup to Lisa's nose. "It's got peach schnapps in it."

Lisa sniffed the cup and smiled half-heartedly. "Mmmm... It smells... peachy. I don't want any, though. Thanks."

Phebe turned around and said confidently, "Kaley! Peach schnapps!" Then she went to everyone she saw and offered, "Peach schnapps? Here's some peach schnapps! We've got a lot of peach schnapps!"

Joanna leaned to Lisa and whispered, "She is being sooooo show-offy tonight! What's with all this confidence with the booze?"

Lisa rolled her eyes in agreement. "Geez, I think she just said *peach schnapps* about thirty times in the last three minutes."

"If the cops show up but we're *not* drinking, do we still get in trouble?"

"I don't know. Probably."

As Phebe carried around her cup of peach schnapps, someone came up and handed her a large dark bottle of some kind of liquor. Joanna couldn't read the label from where she was sitting, but it wouldn't have mattered anyway since she didn't know anything about any kinds of liquor. Phebe set the cup down, grabbed the neck of the bottle, and tipped it back into her mouth.

"Look at her!" Joanna exclaimed in a whisper to Lisa, sitting up straighter and feeling the pit in her stomach quadruple in size. "She is going to be dead after gulping all of that!"

"What is it?" Lisa wondered.

"I don't know, but it can't be good."

"We've gotta take her home. She's gonna kill herself."

"Ughhh. I'm going to throw up," Joanna moaned. "And *not* because I'm drunk!"

Dana Strohbeck was now carrying around a cup that she kept refilling with... something. She and Pelin were stumbling around and laughing.

"What's with the *flower*?" Pelin asked Dana playfully, putting her arm around her and grabbing at her cup. There was a black scribbly flower drawn on the cup with a Sharpie. Pelin's long, dark hair was messy and matted around her face.

Dana laughed and explained, "That's *my* flower on *my* cuppie! It's so you know it's *mine* and you don't get my *germs.*"

"Robbie said he's going to *de-flower* you tonight, Dana," Pelin slurred happily, looking her friend closely in the eye.

"Ohhhh... my flower's been dee'd a long time ago, Pee-Pee, you know that!" Dana announced. "Like, *long* ago!"

Pelin giggled. "Make sure you wear a rain coat, so you don't get any germs from Robbie's pee-pee." Then she whispered dramatically, "And don't do it in my room. Go in my brother's and lock the door."

Joanna sat up straighter then. "Did you drive here?" she asked Lisa hopefully, even though she remembered Kaley saying earlier that Lisa would come with her.

"No, I rode with the Saints," Lisa said, confirming Joanna's memory. "I wish I did, though, because then I could leave. I don't think it's a good idea to be here."

Joanna looked desperately around the room. "Do you think *anyone* here is going to leave before they are wasted?"

"*Nnnn-ope.*"

"Nathan's supposed to be my ride home," Joanna told her, slumping back down into the corner of the couch. "This was supposed to be our date, but look at this mess! There's no way he can drive! He's bombed!"

Phebe came back to the couch and said, "Who, Nathan? He's not bombed, Joanna. Don't be so dramatic. He's just a little buzzed."

Joanna studied her best friend curiously. Other than the over-confidence, Phebe didn't seem the least bit affected by the alcohol. "How are *you* even still alive?" Joanna asked her.

Phebe scrunched her face in confusion. "What do you mean?"

"You just downed like half a bottle of something over there!" Joanna cried. "How can you not be dead?"

Phebe smiled and winked in triumph. "Jay, you just have to know how to play the game." She leaned close and whispered fiercely, "You stick your tongue in the head of the bottle to plug it when you tip it back. I didn't drink any of it. But I looked pretty cool *as if*, didn't I?" She smiled proudly. "You should try it." Then she walked away to the other room with her fancy cup of peach schnapps.

Joanna fell back on the couch and breathed a sigh of relief. Of course Phebe would have a way around all of this. Phebe was an expert at pulling off 'cool.'

People were getting louder, and Nathan was getting more boisterous. Joanna wondered if he was annoyed with her for not joining in on the "fun," but she didn't care. She wanted out of there. She stood up finally and said to Lisa, "I'm calling my house and going home. My parents will come get me and I'll be the big lame dork, and I'll probably get in trouble, but I'm not going to get arrested when this place gets raided by the cops. I can't be a teacher with an arrest record."

Lisa followed her as she walked into the den. There was no one else in that room, and there was a telephone on the desk. It looked like a business phone, but Joanna hoped it would make 'normal' calls – quickly – before anyone saw what she was doing.

Joanna dialed her home phone number, and when Mr. Conors answered, she said, "Dad! Hi Dad... Is Jodie home? Can I talk to Jodie?" She figured her sister could help. Jodie had her license now... Maybe she could come pick her up...

"What's going on, Joanna-Bear? Jodie's in bed."

Well, that wasn't going to work. Joanna had no choice but to just get right to the point. "Dad... I need a ride home. Can you come get me?"

There was a pause, and then her father said, "Yes... Sure, Joanna-Bear. Are you at the billiards place?"

"No... I'm at Pelin's house. A girl from Poms." She turned to Lisa and whispered, "What's the address here?"

Lisa shrugged and shook her head.

Joanna turned back to the phone. "Daddy, I'm sorry, I don't know the address, but just please come!"

"Well, Joanna, I need an address –"

"Maple Street!" Lisa whispered fiercely, hitting Joanna's arm in the dark. "We're on Maple Street! Just down the block from Len's!"

"Dad, it's in town, on Maple Street just past Len's," she said, referring to the little market known for the mural on its brick outside wall. "It's like five houses past Len's. I'll come outside and meet you at the market. Just go to Len's."

Some people walked by in the hallway past the den as Joanna hung up the phone. "I'm leaving," she announced quietly to Lisa as she walked out of the dark room.

"Can I come with you?" Lisa asked her hopefully, following her. The girls smelled cigarette smoke from the family room, and Joanna looked down at the table near the front door. She remembered that Nathan's car keys for the Camaro were in her pocket; he had given them to her after he popped his trunk, so that he could carry his box of liquor with both hands.

"Yes," she answered Lisa. There was a notepad and a pen on the table, next to a vase with fake flowers in it. Joanna picked up the pen and quickly wrote on the notepad:

> Lisa & I left early, so no worries about giving us a ride home. Thanks for the fun party! ♡ Joanna
>
> P.S. I have Nathan's car keys – I will bring them back Sunday morning. Stay safe!

The girls went outside and walked up the street, freezing, but glad to be out of Pelin's house. Within minutes, Mr. Conors pulled up, and they climbed into the car.

"Lisa's coming too," Joanna said hurriedly as she buckled her seat belt and sighed with relief. Lisa settled into the back seat and rubbed her cold hands together.

"That's fine," Mr. Conors replied. "Your brother comin' too?"

"He didn't come to the party. He stayed at Riverside with Matthew and Nicole. He is riding home with Matthew." Joanna was glad to be confident in her information about her brother, since she didn't have any answers about her own situation.

"So... How'd you end up here?"

Joanna sighed. "Dad... I'm sorry. We were at Riverside, and then everyone decided they were going to Pelin's house, and Kaley – this other girl we know – told me Christopher was coming too but he didn't, but... Well, once we got there I just wanted to leave. So, thank you for coming to get us."

"Mmm-hmmm." Mr. Conors flicked on his blinker as he approached the intersection. "Are Pelin's parents home?"

"No, sir," Joanna answered quietly.

"Did you know that before you went there?" he asked, indirectly referencing the Conors family rule about teenager parties requiring parental supervision. This rule often made Joanna feel alienated, but right now, she completely understood why her parents enforced it.

"I think someone said that her parents might not be there, but I was riding with Nathan and he wanted me to go and..." The more Joanna elaborated on this, the more she realized how silly she sounded. Her father was not going to buy any excuses, so she just stopped talking.

Mr. Conors nodded and said, "I suppose you got there and they had alcohol."

"Yes, sir." Her response was barely above a whisper.

Mr. Conors was again silent for a moment, but then he said, "Well, you did the right thing, Joanna Bear, by calling for us to come get you. I'm proud of you girls for doing the right thing."

I'm getting scared, Herr Journal. Maybe Nathan isn't a good match for me. He really likes to drink, and I'm not quite there yet. He's probably going to be so mad when he finds out I took his car keys... but I wouldn't be able to live with myself if he drove home drunk and killed himself or someone else.

Chapter 17: Prom Plans

On Monday morning at school, Nathan met up with Joanna at her locker before first hour. "Hey," he said sweetly.

"Oh, hi," she said. She wasn't sure what had happened at the rest of the party, or how Nathan had reacted when he found out his keys were gone. Early that next morning, she had driven over to Pelin's house, and after seeing Nathan's car still parked up the street, she left the keys in an envelope on Pelin's front steps. She rang the doorbell and disappeared before anyone answered. She didn't talk to anyone from school all day on Sunday, including Phebe, who Joanna assumed would be annoyed and probably mad at her.

Now that she was back at school, Joanna suddenly became nervous, so she said, "I'm sorry I bailed on Saturday. I wasn't feeling well, and... well, I was worried that someone might try to take your car."

Nathan chuckled. "It's alright, Joanna." He quickly kissed the top of her head, and she breathed a sigh of relief. Homeroom and English Lit would be pretty awkward if Nathan was mad at her. "Man!" he went on. "Yesterday was a little rough though!" They started to walk down the hall, and he asked her, "Do you want to come over after school today and study for our Econ test?"

"Okay," Joanna said. Studying for a test would be a safe date, she decided. It was only the parties that she worried about.

Phebe ran up to them then, and declared, "You missed *everything* when you bailed at the party, Jay."

Nathan quickly pulled Joanna into a sideways hug, kissed her on the cheek, and whispered in her ear, "I'll see ya in a few minutes, sweetheart. I gotta run to the can before class." He darted into the bathroom.

"You missed everything!" Phebe repeated. "Violet puked, Blake puked, *everybody* puked except me and Shana. Dana had sex with one of Pelin's brother's friends! The really hot blond dude. Everyone was listening to them outside the bedroom door! And there are rumors that *Kaley* gave Ryan Staeffer a —" she stopped and cleared her throat, hoping to communicate what that certain activity was with just her eyes. Then she continued, "—in the laundry room, but I haven't verified this yet..."

Joanna was walking a little faster than Phebe just to stay ahead of her, and she waved her hand in dismissal. "I don't really want to know any of this, Phebe!" she called behind her.

"Everyone thinks you're lame for leaving," Phebe grumbled after her.

Joanna stopped and turned around. "Everyone was too drunk to notice, I'm sure."

"Well, you left a note!"

"I *know*! That was so that when you all woke up after puking and passing out, Nathan would know where his car keys were! I thought that was pretty nice of us to leave a note."

"Well, we all just slept over there anyway," Phebe muttered. "Nobody was driving."

"Great. You're in with the cool kids now. Congratulations."

"Are you *never* going to drink, Joanna? Because that's what people do at our age. You're really going to look like a lame duck if you bail at parties like that."

Joanna shrugged her shoulders. "So, I'm a lame duck. Fine." She left Phebe in the hallway and walked into her classroom.

Joanna thought about this as she sat down in her Homeroom class. *A lame duck. I am the dorky little goody-goody who ran away from the big scary party. But what does it matter? Pom season is over now, so I don't have to associate with Pelin or Dana anymore.* There were literally only nine weeks left of school. No more hockey games or Poms. If only she could keep Nathan away from the parties, life would be perfect.

***

Nathan continued to dote on Joanna at school and on weekends. There weren't any more parties like Joanna feared, so things with her social life fell back into place. Nathan was as sweet as ever, and he ate lunch at Joanna's table with her group more often than he did with his louder guy group. Joanna really felt like she was in love. There were no more incidents with drinking, so she hoped maybe her boyfriend had gotten it out of his system.

One day in April, Nicole slid next to Joanna at lunch and said excitedly, "Prom tickets go on sale tomorrow! Just think Joanna, we'll get to go to Prom together!"

Joanna looked up from her cheese quesadilla and smiled. "Yeah! That's true! If Nathan will take me!"

"Well, of course he'll take you!" Nicole laughed. "He's your boyfriend!"

The next day at lunch, Senior Prom was the hot topic of discussion. Nathan and Christopher both bought their tickets, and suddenly everyone else at the table decided that they all wanted to go, even if they all just paired up as friends. Aaron Mickels asked Phebe, who immediately agreed. And even Lisa, for whom money was tight and would probably have to borrow a dress, agreed to go with another friend in their group, Blake Markoff.

Laura Vigent had been sitting with the crew all semester, but even after all these weeks, she was still shy and awkward. She was pleasant, and nobody minded her presence, but she was quiet and hadn't seemed to have reached her comfort level within the group yet. On the day of the prom discussion, just to make conversation, Joanna turned to Laura and said quietly, "Would you go to Prom if someone asked you? Even just as friends?"

Laura shifted uncomfortably, but smiled with a hint of intrigue in her eyes. "Ohhh, I don't know. I never really thought about it!"

"Well, do you like anyone? Do you have any guy buddies that you would go with?"

Laura didn't answer right away, but Joanna could tell she was thinking about it now.

Then Laura smiled. Her tone indicated trust in Joanna as she said softly, "Well... I kind of like Matthew. He's such a nice guy. Does he have a date?"

Hmmm. Joanna kind of liked this idea. If Matthew went with Laura, then he'd be able to go to the dance with all of their friends! Joanna wanted Matthew to be there; their friend group wasn't the same without him. And Laura was safe. She was boring and simple, and it would just be a formality of them pairing up, so that they both could attend.

Just then, Nathan came over to Joanna from behind and kissed her on the cheek. He grabbed a grape from her lunch tray, popped it in his mouth, and said, "Hey, Cutie." He wrapped his arms around her shoulders.

Joanna turned to get herself out of the bench. "Hi." She wondered if she should use an affectionate nickname for her beau. After all, that's what boyfriends and girlfriends were supposed to do, right? So, she quickly added, "Honeybuns." Then she turned back to Laura and stood up. "Laura, I don't know if Matthew has anyone in mind for a date. But I'll find out!"

That afternoon, Joanna rode with Matthew to the Toy Store after school, since they both would be working that night. "So, Matthew," she said to him casually, once they got on the main road heading to the shopping center. "Are you going to Prom?"

"Aw, probably not," he replied.

"Well, I feel bad!" she said. "All of us in our group are going! We gotta find dates for you and Colvin."

Matthew scrunched up his face and shook his head. "Nah. Who would we go with, anyway? It'd be too awkward."

"Well, what if someone wanted to go with you? Would you go if you had a date?"

"Why, who wants to go with me?" he asked her. "And please don't say Phebe."

Joanna giggled and rolled her eyes playfully. "No, no, Phebe is *sooooo* over you, boy. She's going with Aaron, remember? But I know of someone who is interested in going with you, just as a friend, if you wanted to go."

"Who?"

Joanna paused. "Laura Vigent."

Matthew looked a little taken aback. "Laura? Lunch table Laura? The Laura that doesn't talk to anyone?"

"She's really sweet," Joanna defended her. "She's just quiet. She's super smart though, and nice. I think you should ask her." Joanna thought about

After Tomorrow

Laura. Poor, quiet Laura, who probably never had a guy flirt with her in her whole life. How sweet it would be for her to have a nice guy like Matthew give her the experience of going to her Senior Prom.

And how sweet for Matthew to be able to go also, since he didn't have a real girlfriend. "Then you could be there with all of us," Joanna coaxed him. "After all, Matthew, this is our *Senior Prom!*"

Matthew didn't seem interested. "I don't know, Jay. I guess I'll think about it."

A few days later, Joanna followed up with Matthew during History class. "So? You gonna ask Laura to Prom?"

"I don't know. Yeah, sure, I guess."

Then that same day, in sixth hour pre-calc, Laura ran up to Joanna and cried, "Guess what, Joanna! Matthew asked me to go to Prom with him!"

"Really?" Joanna exclaimed. This was the most excitement she had ever seen from Laura. "That's wonderful!"

***

That afternoon when Joanna got home from school, she looked in the fridge and saw the half-empty 16-ounce bottle of AquaJest purified drinking water that she had opened the day before. She grabbed the bottle and looked at the light-blue label; purified drinking water sold in a bottle was a relatively new concept, and AquaJest had recently hit the market in Woodland Hills.

You stick your tongue in the head of the bottle to plug it when you tip it back, she remembered Phebe saying at the party. Joanna unscrewed the plastic cap. If she could learn how to fake slamming a bottle of liquor at parties, she might be set to survive the rest of senior year.

> Matthew is going to have Laura be his date for Prom, Herr Journal. This is good, so now he can be there with us! He doesn't really like her, by the way, but you have to have a date to go to Prom. Problem solved! ☺

Chapter 18: It's Over

Life appeared to be going well for Joanna in the social department. She must have become 'cool' again, or maybe it was that Phebe had become less obsessed with being 'cool,' and their *Freundschaft* was back on track. Now that everyone had dates for Prom, everyone was 'cool.'

Nathan was sweet to Joanna, and she loved kissing him. Kissing is as far as she would go, and that seemed to be okay with him. Occasionally he would hint that they should do a little more, but he never badgered her.

At least, he never badgered her when he was sober.

Though there were fewer parties, Nathan still found occasion to drink, and that's when he'd ask Joanna to do more with him. He wanted her to drink with him, and he wanted her to do things with his body that he knew other girls were doing with their boyfriends' bodies.

Joanna tried very hard to become comfortable with alcohol, but it was a slow process. So slow, in fact, that it really wasn't happening. When she and Nathan studied together after school, Nathan would fix himself a Tom Collins, his favorite cocktail. Or he'd crack open a can of beer. Or he'd have both! His parents were never home; they were always at the Lure managing their business.

"Can't a man fix his woman a drink?" he'd ask her. "You make me feel like a cheap host!"

"I'm good, Honeybuns," she'd reply with an uncomfortable, forced smile. She always tried to change the subject, but often he became relentless when suggesting that they fool around a bit.

He'd get close to her, and she could smell the booze on his breath. "The hard stuff will help you relax, babe. They don't call it liquid courage for nothin'!"

Study dates like this were becoming the norm.

"I'm not saying he's an alcoholic," Lisa told Joanna carefully once, when Joanna had confided her concerns about the drinking. "But this is exactly my mother. Can't go a day without a drink, sweet as ever when she feels guilty about it..." Lisa never talked much about her mother's alcoholism, but she also never denied the reality of the situation with Joanna. The Conors family had been Lisa's safe haven too many times to count over the years.

"So he *is* an alcoholic," Joanna had confirmed, when Lisa brought it up.

Lisa just hugged her friend and said gently, "He could be on that path."

Joanna tried to ignore the nagging feeling that Lisa was right. She constantly told herself that Nathan was just going through a phase of experimentation with booze and having a girlfriend, and the novelty would soon wear off. *He's just so young!* she thought. *Young people drink. That's just the nature of their foolishness at this age. Alcoholics are the old people who can't control it.*

But Lisa had advised, "Even if he outgrows it eventually, this is where he is *now.* Is this what you want in your life *right now?*"

Lisa was very wise.

***

Mr. Simon, the economics teacher, had his students work in small groups during class one day. Pelin scooted her chair closer to Nathan's desk and asked, "You gonna be ready for a big one this weekend?" The other students shifted their seats around the room to form small pods of two or three.

Lisa was nearby, joined with Laura Vigent and another classmate. Being on the pom squad with Pelin and being one of Joanna's best friends might suggested that Lisa would have grouped herself with Pelin and Nathan. Nathan would have welcomed her, but Lisa was frankly not a fan of Pelin's. And these days, she was a bit wary about Nathan, too. Being with Laura was more comfortable.

But Lisa listened intently to the conversation going on behind her, as she dug in her purse for a pen.

"Ohhhhh yeah," Nathan confirmed, leaning back in his chair and combing his fingers through his short, dark hair.

"Your little *princess* gonna be there?"

"I don't think she'll come. She's not too big on the drinking."

Pelin just looked at Nathan, and then asked bluntly, almost accusingly, "Why are you dating her?"

Nathan sat straight in his chair, and then leaned forward as he folded his hands together on his desk. "I like her! She's cool. She's mysterious." Then he broke into the tune of a popular radio hit: *"She's cool, in myster-ious ways, ohh-oh."*

Pelin rolled her eyes. "That's not how the song goes."

"Well, she's cool and I like her. She's my type."

"You're never gonna get any from her, you know."

"Pelin, that's not yours to worry about, okay?"

"I'm just sayin'. She lives in the Virgin Vault, and that's not likely to open anytime soon."

Nathan just smiled and said, "Well, you never know."

✳✳✳

After dress shopping at a mall in the Twin Cities all afternoon, Joanna and Phebe wrapped up their Saturday with some pizza at the food court. The trek back to Woodland Hills would take close to an hour, and it was getting late.

"We should bring some of this pizza back for Nathan," Joanna suggested, suddenly hoping to see her boyfriend after a long day up in the Cities.

Since Joanna was the one to bring up Nathan's name, Phebe asked casually, "Is there a party tonight?"

Joanna thought for a moment. "No... I don't think so." But her instincts kicked in; she could feel her heart jump a bit closer to her throat.

"I think there might be." The contradiction was delicate.

Since experience had shown Phebe's social radar to be consistently accurate, Joanna's heart now sank. "He didn't mention having any plans this weekend..."

Unable to keep pertinent information from her best friend, Phebe said bluntly, "Yeah, well, Lisa overheard them talking about a party. She wasn't sure if she should tell you... Well, you know. In case it wasn't true. Or whatever."

Joanna didn't waste time pondering any emotions that might be stirred when learning that her two best friends now seemed to know more about her boyfriend than she did. She cut right to the chase. "He drinks too much, Phebe. Don't you think so?"

"Yeah! I do think so!"

"Well, then why do you always harp on me just because I don't like being around drinking?"

"I'm not harping on you, Jay. I don't like all the drinking either. I just think you need to fake it a little better so they don't think we're a bunch of dorks."

"Well, I don't care if *they* think we're a bunch of dorks. I think *they're* a bunch of losers!"

Phebe sighed, falling to the support of her elbows on the table. "So, Nathan never mentioned this party?"

Joanna sighed too. "I don't think he even tells me anymore if there is one. He knows I won't want to go."

"Why are you dating him?" Phebe asked bluntly.

The question took Joanna by surprise. She never imagined Phebe would ask her such a thing, so she replied with the only answer she knew: "Because... he's the most popular guy in school, and he asked me out, so... wouldn't I be crazy *not* to date him?"

Phebe didn't seem to have answers either. "Well, it just... It just doesn't seem like it's working. Is this how dating is supposed to be?"

"I don't know, Phebe! I don't know anything about dating anyone! Every girl in the school seems to think Nathan Hooks is the big catch, so who am I to throw that away just because he likes to drink? Am I, Little Miss Middle-Class Goody-Goody, even *allowed* to dump him? Shouldn't *he* be dumping *me* when he finally decides I'm too boring?"

"I don't know!"

"Well, I don't know either! And how is that going to look? Can you even imagine the buzz around town? *What? Joanna Conors dumped Nathan Hooks?? Who does she think she is?*"

"And you hate to throw away someone like Nathan Hooks just because of this temporary phase he's going through, right?" Phebe advised, though her suggestion lacked confidence. "I mean, this drinking thing is just a phase, right? And he probably feels a lot of pressure from all his buddies..."

"Well, now we're making excuses, Pheebs." Joanna thought about what Lisa had said to her earlier, about it not mattering if Nathan will eventually "outgrow" this "phase." This is how he is *now*. "I don't think I have time for this in my life. I can't even believe I've succumbed to all this nonsense."

After pondering a moment, Phebe jumped up. "Let's bring him the pizza! He's supposedly not doing anything tonight, right??"

***

Nathan's family was quite well-off, and his parents' home was up in the true "hills" of Woodland Hills. "The Hills" was where all the affluent families resided, in vast homes with large windows, brick walkways, and professional landscaping. Most of the residents were small business owners in town, or investors and corporate heads that worked up in the Twin Cities.

"So, this is how the other half lives," Phebe commented, as she drove the two of them along the winding, wooded roads lined with mansions.

"Yep," Joanna confirmed, concentrating to make sure the directions she was giving Phebe were correct. She strained to remember the way to Nathan's house, as she had only driven out this way once by herself. The other times, he had always picked her up.

Phebe shook her head. "I've lived in this town my whole life, and I've never gone up here into the Hills."

"Same. I never came up here until Nathan."

"Man, what do these people *do* to afford homes like this??"

"I don't know. They must all be attorneys or on-call doctors, or corporate people that spend all their time at their office and commuting, because it never seems like anyone is ever home," Joanna said. "Or, in Nathan's parents' case, they practically live at their bar because they have to be there all the time to run it." She saw the trees that arched across the property at the end of the Hooks' driveway. "That's it," she said.

Phebe turned in, and pulled close to the attached three-car garage. The girls walked up the brick pathway lined with small, round garden lights. "I know you said he lives in a mansion," Phebe commented, "but I guess I didn't realize it really *is* a mansion!"

"Yep. The custodian at our school cleans their windows on the weekends."

"No kidding! Diego?"

"Yeah. It's like a side job or something. Dustin Rollick lives up in these hills here somewhere too, you know. Diego also cleans the Rollicks' windows, and the windows of some other houses around here. He's, like, the weekend window guy. It's probably a pretty good side gig, if you have the equipment to get way up *there*."

Phebe eyed all of the windows on just the front of the house, trying to imagine how many more were around the sides and back. "Yeah, I suppose it'd be impossible to wash all of these yourself. But who washes windows, anyway?? I don't think my parents have ever washed our windows!"

"People with money do!"

"I always wondered why Nathan sometimes talks to Diego at school when he's emptying the trash after lunch or whatever. I thought he was just being Mr. Friendly who talks to everyone."

"Well, he is being Mr. Friendly who talks to everyone," Joanna said, "but it's also because Diego washes his windows on the weekends." She pressed the button for the electronic doorbell. "Dustin Rollick won't talk to Diego; he thinks Diego is trash," she went on while they waited. "Typical jerkoid Rollick. Too good for the common man."

Phebe looked around the neighborhood. The homes were spaced apart, with curved pathways, low walls made of stone, impeccable groundskeeping, and illuminated topiaries. "Wow, I had no idea *this* exists in Woodland Hills!"

Joanna pointed in the direction farther down the winding road. "Those homes up that way overlook Lake W. I'm pretty sure Dana lives somewhere up there. And Grant McAllister lives in the rich-but-not-*as*-rich part."

"How did Pelin get in with this group when she lives in a normal house on Maple Street?" Now Phebe was really interested the lives of the Woodland Hills version of the Rich and Famous.

Joanna shrugged. "Everyone else lives in town. It's only Nathan and those other three that live up here in the Hills."

The door to the enormous Hooks estate opened. Nathan was home alone; his parents would be at the Lure all night again. But as soon as Joanna and Phebe stepped into the massive foyer, they could tell Nathan had been drinking. He seemed surprised, but happy, to see the girls. "Hey-ey! M'two favorite babes!"

"You reek like alcohol," Phebe said bluntly to him, as she walked through the entry and found her way to the kitchen. She reached across the colossal island and picked up a bottle of tequila. Though she had never been there before, she made herself at home.

"I'm... juss gettin' ready for when m'boys come over lay-*ter*," he slurred happily. And sure enough, within the hour, several guys from their class all showed up and were ready to party.

Pelin and Dana also arrived, together.

"Girls!" Udo Meikler exclaimed as he walked through the front sitting room, when he saw his classmates in the kitchen. "You girls gonna party with us tonight? Pheebs, we can get you some Peach Schnapps!"

"Yeah, maybe," Phebe said coolly. She hoisted herself up to sit on the marble countertop, next to the sink.

Pelin eyed Nathan. He caught her glance, which quickly turned into a smirk.

Nathan took the cue and walked right up to Joanna. Joanna was not dressed for a party, but her mid-rise, flared jeans fit her long legs and slender hips perfectly, and the casual sag of her navy Liberty High School hoodie confirmed that she actually was *cool*. Her not trying to be cool made her cool after all.

The slice of Pelin's stare tore at Joanna, as Nathan rubbed his hands up and down his girlfriend's arms. He looked seductively into her face. "Maybe *my* baby will *par-tay* with me tonight. What d'you think, Babe? As soon as these guys all get settled," he leaned into her ear and whispered, "we can go upstairs and have our own" – he licked her earlobe – "little," – he licked it again as she squirmed – "private party..."

Joanna stepped back, her heart now in her throat. The alcohol on his breath confirmed with his actions that her boyfriend was beyond buzzed. He had never come onto her so strong as he did now; he was a whole different person. Ignoring Pelin's dagger-eyes, she gently pushed Nathan away from her. "I don't think I can stay."

Joanna and Phebe didn't leave right away, but they relocated to a couch and hung around for another hour, watching as more people showed up for the party. Most of the guests were from school, but there were a few others that they didn't recognize. Nathan's inebriation frightened Joanna. It scared her more than the slight discomfort she had felt in the past. Nathan was loud and belligerent, and Joanna suspected, based on the non-reaction of everyone else, that this was not unusual behavior for him when he played with alcohol.

Phebe didn't drink that night. In fact, even she seemed bothered this time by the severity of the behaviors they were witnessing, and she leaned back against the couch with a big sigh. "This is kind of scary, Jay," she admitted.

"How did all these people know about this party?" Joanna pondered to Phebe, who was likely now the only other sober person in the house. "We never heard about it. Even if he knew I wouldn't want to come, you'd think for a party this big, my *boyfriend* would have wanted me here!"

"Look around," Phebe pointed out. "It's all the drinkers from school. No one from our group. I've never seen half these people before! They must be from Middleton." Middleton was the other high school, a smaller school located between Woodland Hills and Cannon Valley that served students from both towns.

Before long, people were spilling things, tripping over furniture, and throwing up. Two girls were crying, but nobody knew why. One guy was making out with two girls on the floor in the corner.

"I hate to say this, Pheebs," Joanna sighed sadly, "but it's over. I can't deal with this. I don't want to be a girlfriend to this."

"This *is* pretty bad," Phebe agreed. Joanna was surprised at Phebe's new reservation towards all the drinking and 'being cool,' but Phebe explained, "It's like I've said before, Jay. You have to play the game. I don't like any of this drinking and puking and all that either. You have to fake it enough while they're sober enough to see you being part of it, and then get out of it once everyone else is bombed. Then you won't look like such a goody-two-shoes." Phebe sure knew how to play the game.

Joanna didn't say anything. She was certain that nobody even knew she and Phebe were there right now, but then Nathan came over to them and pulled Joanna up by the hand. "C'mon, woman! The guys are tellin' me it's about time I get laid!"

In a sudden surge of confidence, Phebe jumped up to Nathan and looked closely into his eyes. "You're so freakin' drunk," she told him boldly. "Do you really think *Joanna Conors* is going to waste her time with a *drunk*? Good God, Nathan, she's heading to UW-Timberwood in the fall! Who do you think you are?"

"Nathan, we're going to go," Joanna said in a tone far less igniting than Phebe's. She pulled Phebe away. But Nathan wasn't hearing anything. He started dancing around, and he grabbed the TV remote. At first, he started singing into it as if it were a microphone, and a few people laughed. Nathan clearly liked to be the center of attention at parties.

Joanna and Phebe headed through the foyer to the front door, and Nathan yelled playfully, "Hey, bimbos! Where you goin'?" A few of the other guys laughed.

Joanna couldn't get the handle on the door to unlatch right away, and Nathan yelled, "Hey, Woman! Don't leave my par-tay!"

This time his voice was angry.

Ryan Staeffer, a classmate, scoffed, "She's leavin' you, man! You ain't gettin' *any* action tonight!"

"My hot babe ain't gonna leave my par-tay!" Nathan yelled. He threw the remote right at Joanna, and it hit her at the side of her eye.

When Joanna got the door open, Phebe pushed her outside. "Go, Jay! Just go!" The two girls ran along the lighted brick pathway and got into Phebe's car; thankfully no one had parked them in. As she started the engine, they saw Nathan in the front doorway yelling something at them, but they drove off before deciphering what it was.

"What a jackass!" Phebe exclaimed, gripping the steering wheel angrily. "Are you okay? Did that thing hit you?"

"Yes!" Joanna cried, rubbing the side of her eye. She pulled the visor down to check the mirror. The side of her face had a slight red mark on it. Then she grabbed Phebe's arm. "Slow down. There's a speed limit on these streets and they'll catch you." The girls were quiet for a moment, as Phebe slowed her driving to accommodate the law. Then Joanna said incredulously, "UW-*Timberwood*, Phebe??"

"Yeah, what about it?" Phebe replied, keeping her eyes on the winding road and her hands gripped tightly to the steering wheel.

Joanna almost laughed. "You announced that like it was... I don't know, important or prestigious or something!"

Phebe giggled now too. "Yeah, so?"

Joanna was confused, but laughed again. "Well! I don't get it! Why'd you say that like that?"

"Because he needs to wake up and see what he's gonna lose!"

"UW-Timberwood is a state school, Phebe, not Ivy League!"

After Tomorrow

"Yeah, well, whatever. I had to say something. They were all drunk anyway."

Then the realization of what had just happened hit Joanna, and she burst into tears. "I can't believe it's over, Phebe!"

"We'll figure this out, Jay," Phebe assured her when they got out to the main road. "Where should we go?"

Joanna was all-out crying now. "I don't know! I can't go home like this!" She buried her face in her hands.

"Okay. Let's see if Matthew's home." They drove back towards town, to the Carmichaels' house and pulled into their driveway.

Matthew answered the door himself, and invited the girls in. His parents were out.

When Joanna came inside, Matthew immediately put his hands on her shoulders and asked with concern, "Jay! What's wrong?"

It didn't take long for the girls to tell the story. Joanna cried the whole time while they sat at the kitchen table, and Matthew made them some warm apple cider. Joanna loved Mrs. Carmichael's warm apple cider, and Matthew did a pretty good job of replicating it for his guests.

"So much for my wonderful *boyfriend*," Joanna said softly, once she finally stopped crying. The three friends hung out for a while longer, contemplating all of Joanna's options.

"Just call him up tomorrow and tell him to go to hell," Phebe suggested protectively.

Matthew, taking a more civil approach, advised, "No, no, no. Next time you see him, when he's sober, just *inform* him that since you guys are not a match, you won't be dating him anymore."

"How did I not see this?" Joanna wondered desperately, slamming her elbows to the table and shoving her hands along the sides of her face. "I mean, this clearly wasn't the first time he was *that* sloshed!"

Matthew put his arm gently around her shoulders. "You didn't want to see it, Jay."

***

Christopher's reaction, however, later that night when Joanna got home, was more aggressive. "He hit you?" he cried accusingly.

Joanna sighed. "*He* didn't hit me. The remote did."

"He *threw* a *remote* at you?"

Now the tears started up again, as Joanna cried, "You're not making this any easier, Big Brother!"

"You did the right thing, Sweet Pea," her mother told her the next day, when they sat in Joanna's bedroom and talked about it. "It's disappointing, I know, that he can be such a great guy and then throw everything away with the alcohol, but it's better you realize this now, rather than after you've invested even more of your heart into him."

"I guess it's time to make the phone call, then," Joanna sighed. "Is it okay to do it over the phone?" Breaking up with someone was something Joanna hadn't done before, and she wasn't even sure of the protocol. Her mother nodded, then left the room so she'd have privacy.

When Nathan answered the phone, Joanna took a deep breath, and then just spit out the lines she'd been rehearsing all day. She spoke quickly, and with confidence. "Hi Nathan. I'm calling to let you know that we will no longer be going out, and I am not your girlfriend anymore." She let out the breath that she hadn't realized she was holding. Then she added, "And I think you know why."

There was silence on the other end of the line, but finally Nathan said quietly, "Yeah. Yeah, I guess I do. I don't blame you."

Well, you'd better not blame me, because you're the drunk, Joanna thought bitterly. But aloud she said awkwardly, after a long pause, "Well, good-bye, then. I guess."

"Good-bye, Joanna."

After Tomorrow

***

"I don't blame you??" Phebe cried disgustedly that afternoon when Joanna told her about the phone call. Joanna was over at her house so that they could finish an assignment together. "He wasn't even like, *Oh no! No, I'll change! Just give me one more chance!?* He didn't even try to hold onto you??"

"I'm not waiting around for someone to change, Phebe," Joanna told her defensively. She knew Phebe meant well, but sheesh! She wished Phebe could phrase things a little more sensitively sometimes. "He is who he is. Matthew was right. We're not a match."

"Well, he doesn't realize what he's losing," Phebe muttered after a long pause, and Joanna was glad that now Phebe's loyalty was displaying itself more appropriately. "It's his loss."

"I'm sad though," Joanna said softly, picking at the faded green engraving on her pencil. Sadness seeped from her voice as she pondered wistfully, "Hawaii was so great. I just wish it could be like it was in Hawaii."

Phebe put her arm around her best friend and assured her, "It will be, someday. With someone better. Not a drunk."

***

Joanna dialed a number she had dialed a million times before, and when Lisa answered the phone, she opened with a simple, "Hey." She figured she should tell Lisa about the break up herself, before the Liberty High School Gossip Ring snagged her in the morning.

Lisa knew Joanna's voice, and she could tell right away that this call probably wasn't about homework.

"So, I broke up with Nathan," Joanna told her with a sigh. "I guess you could say I dumped him, or whatever they say when you end the relationship." Lisa just listened, so Joanna started to ramble. "I just can't deal with all the drinking, Lisa! I just don't think I'm ready for any of this. It was a lot easier when I was just me. Single. Too many busy-bodies get in your business when you're dating someone. And, we're not a match anyway!" she added, quoting Matthew. "I mean... yeah, we're just not a match."

When Joanna finally took a breath, Lisa said, "I wish I could give you a hug right now. I'm sorry it didn't work out."

"Yeah." Joanna calmed down, once she recognized that Lisa wasn't going to challenge her.

"I'll meet up with you by the wall in the morning if you want to walk into the building together," Lisa offered. "I mean... if you think it might be awkward or whatever... I'm sure word will travel fast."

"Yeah, sure. That'd be good!"

Lisa was great. Always so kind.

✳✳✳

And word did travel fast. As soon as Joanna got to her locker the next morning, Nicole ran up to her, hugged her, and cried, "Joanna! I'm *so sorry* to hear about Nathan!"

"Ohhh, thanks, Nicole," Joanna stammered, although she was a bit surprised by the passion with which Nicole spoke.

"I mean, how awful!" Nicole went on. She kept trying to catch Joanna's eyes, but Joanna continued to fight with her pre-calc textbook that refused to release its grip inside the locker. "This is so *awful*," Nicole continued. "I can't even imagine. I thought you guys would be together forever! I mean..."

"Nicole," Joanna stopped her, finally looked at her, and gently touched her arm. "It's okay. Really."

Nicole paused, and then nodded. "Okay. Well, if you need *anything*..."

Joanna forced a smile of appreciation and said, "Thank you."

✳✳✳

Joanna and Nathan didn't have any classes together other than their homeroom/first hour English, where Nathan just left her alone. Joanna thought about the early days of that semester, when he first joined that class and was seated behind her. He never talked to her back then, when he was blissfully unaware of her existence. Now he didn't talk to her because he was uncomfortable, which was probably best, Joanna decided.

They always seemed to be in the same hallways at the same times, however. Later that first morning when Joanna caught his eyes near the main hall pole, he turned and looked away. One of his buddies came up to him, and then Nathan started to laugh as if he were having the time of his life. Right there in the middle of the main hall during the transition between second and third hour at Liberty High School in Woodland Hills, Minnesota, Nathan Hooks was having the absolute time of his life. With*out* his boring *girlfriend.*

During lunch, Joanna could feel some eyes on her from the "cool" table, but she faced the other way and tried to act like she always had before she was ever dating anyone.

After the last bell of the day, Matthew came up to Joanna. "Hey," he said solemnly, as she hoisted her backpack over her shoulder and they headed toward the main doors to leave. "You doin' okay today? It probably wasn't an easy day with all the buzz about..."

Joanna just shook her head in dismissal as she threw a wad of crumpled old papers from her Economics binder into a recycling barrel when they stepped outside. "It was fine. Nobody really said anything. Or I didn't hear anything, I should say."

"Well, people just like to have something to talk about," Matthew said. "And I heard a few people say nice things! Udo said you're too good for him, and you were smart to move on. And I agree."

"Okay, Matthew. Thank you."

✳✳✳

"So, people have been asking me what the *real* story is about you and Nathan," Phebe announced breathlessly on Tuesday at lunch. She set down her tray, eager to maintain her status as the Chief of Headlines in social drama. Lisa squeezed in next to her.

"Great," Joanna muttered impatiently. "And what, dare I ask, has been your response to that question?" She was already bored with all of this!

Phebe smiled proudly. *"Irreconcilable differences.* You're not a match."

"Okay, great. Because he's Mr. Life-of-the-Party, and I'm the boring Little Miss Goody Two Shoes."

Lisa, always practical, suggested, "Just give it another day or so and everyone will have forgotten that the two of you ever even knew each other's names."

Joanna hoped so. She hated drama!

***

In school later that week, Joanna was in her Economics class when Dustin Rollick said to her, "Why'd you dump Nathan, Joanna? He's heartbroken, you know." His tone was bordering on harassment, as usual, so she ignored him. Dustin Rollick was, frankly, a jerk. He had been harassing Joanna since freshman year of high school, and today was more of the same. He was another one she would not miss once they graduated.

Udo Meikler, who was sitting nearby, said rationally, "Um, I think it's probably because he threw a remote at her and hit her in the face." Though he was the class clown, Udo was never a jerk. He was always very fair and practical with all of his classmates.

"He didn't mean to do that, you know," Dustin tried to justify. "He was just a little drunk. Those things happen when you drink too much."

Dana Strohbeck was sitting in front of Dustin, and she couldn't help putting in her two cents' worth. "Joanna doesn't like drinking. She can't handle... life."

Joanna continued to ignore her peers. She pretended to be reading the article they were assigned, while fighting back tears and feeling her face burn.

After Tomorrow

Why are people such jerks, Herr Journal? I had every right to dump Nathan. He's a drunk. Nothing about all that drinking and partying is impressive to me! Yet I'm made out to be the loser because I'm not 'cool'. Well, Dana and Pelin and Dustin Rollick and all those losers need to just go away. I don't care. They will never amount to anything, at least not morally, so what do I care?

But what about Prom? Now everyone in my group is going except me. Matthew actually joked that he would take me if Laura bailed on him... But Laura's not going to bail on him, and anyway, I can't go with Matthew. If I went with Matthew, everyone would think we like each other. And we don't want people thinking we like each other! Ugh. So, Colvin offered to take me, since he still doesn't have a date either. I guess that won't be the end of the world. At least with Colvin and all of my real friends, I don't have to worry about alcohol. And I certainly don't have to worry about my date wanting to have sex on Prom night!

Chapter 19: Emotions

The night of their Senior Prom came too quickly for Joanna, and she couldn't seem to get a handle on her emotions as Jodie helped her get ready that afternoon.

It shouldn't have bothered Joanna that Matthew was taking Laura Vigent to the dance; after all, Joanna was the one who had set them up! Laura was nothing special. She was plain and quiet and *boring*. Matthew was a nice guy, and he would be a perfect gentleman. And Joanna had her own date – Colvin Jaynort, the simple, affable kid in their friend group – and they were also going just as friends. This shouldn't have been a big deal!

But somehow, it had become a big deal inside Joanna's own head, and now her emotions were getting the best of her.

***

"Here are the bobby pins we need." Jodie entered her sister's room and tossed a small container on the dresser. Joanna stood at her mirror holding all of her curled dark blond hair on top of her head. "Thanks." She turned sideways to look at the back of her teal-colored Lerena Arletta designer original. "Will you finish zipping me up?" The color of the dress accented Joanna's eyes perfectly.

"Are you going to wear your hair up?" Jodie asked as she pulled at her sister's zipper and straightened the ruffle. Many girls from school were going to the upscale salon in town to have their hair professionally done, but Joanna couldn't get an appointment since the arrangement of going to Prom with Colvin came about so late. She had cancelled her original appointment when she broke up with Nathan, assuming then that Prom wasn't going to happen for her. Phebe originally had an appointment at the salon also, but Lisa couldn't afford the salon, so now Phebe cancelled her appointment and the three girls would do their hair together at the Conors' home. Jodie was really good at doing hair, and she couldn't wait to work her magic on her sister and friends for the dance.

Joanna let go of her hair, allowing all of her thick waves to drop around her bare shoulders. "I don't know," she sighed and plopped down on her bed.

"You don't seem like you even want to go!" Jodie commented, plopping down next to her. At sixteen, Jodie wished that she herself were going to the dance, but sophomores couldn't go unless asked by an upperclassman. She could not understand why Joanna, for whom this would be the only prom, did not seem the least bit excited.

Joanna needed a diversion from that comment, so she asked her sister, "Are any people in your class going to Prom?"

"I know of a few girls," Jodie answered. "But not very many. Do you know Tammy Findlerzak? She told everyone she's going to have sex with her boyfriend tonight."

"That's terrible," Joanna commented, staring expressionlessly at the wall. "Whether or not that's her plan, she shouldn't be telling people that."

"I heard her telling Jess Samter that *Robert* had booked a hotel room for them and everything."

"Really?" Joanna challenged her. "And her parents are allowing this?"

"I'm sure they don't know," Jodie guessed. "Tammy said that Robert doesn't want to graduate high school still a virgin, so he picked her to *give his gift to.*"

Joanna rolled her eyes. "Robert? Robert Vanguard in my grade?"

"Yep."

"That figures. He's such a tool. Can't get someone his own age so he's trollin' down to the sophomores."

"Yep."

Joanna's mind wandered for a moment, and she started to think about Nathan. Nathan Hooks, the guy she *should* have been going to Prom with.

She really missed having a "real" boyfriend now, even though she was the one who dumped him. She didn't like to admit that she was afraid of alcohol, and that drinking scared her. Joanna thought about how Nathan's experimentation with alcohol during this last year of school had transformed him into a completely different person, and whenever he drank, he would become obnoxious and somewhat belligerent, hinting to her that they should take their physical relationship to the next level. She knew that even if they had stayed together and were going to Prom now, somehow Nathan would have brought alcohol onto the scene, and that would have stressed Joanna out. Her practical brain knew it was best to not be with Nathan for Prom, but her emotional brain missed the potential of a sweet, romantic night.

Why couldn't this be like Hawaii??

Earlier that morning, Joanna jotted down a few thoughts in her journal to try to calm her mind:

> It's good that Nathan and I aren't going to Prom together. He probably would have wanted us to have sex since he'd be drinking, or to prove something to his buddies. Or he'd be super loud and obnoxious about it around everyone else. Or he'd be so drunk off his butt all night that he'd probably get arrested for doing something stupid. Or... or... or... The risks are countless!

Yes, it was surely best to be done with Nathan Hooks, but that didn't make things any easier as she was getting ready for the dance.

Joanna thought about her brother and his girlfriend, Nicole. Christopher and Nicole were still going strong. They were the only serious couple in the group going to Prom. Joanna knew that Nicole's value system – and also Christopher's – precluded having premarital sex, but she couldn't help wondering if those values would be challenged under the right circumstances. After all, it was Prom Night.

Almost as if reading her mind, Jodie interrupted Joanna's thoughts by saying, "*You* aren't going to have sex tonight, just because it's Prom night, are you Jo-Jo?" Her tone had a hint of worry in it.

Joanna looked at her sister, a bit astonished. When everything with Nathan unraveled, Colvin was the only one in the group who didn't have a date yet for Prom. Since everyone was pairing up as friends, Colvin agreed to take Joanna as his date.

"Colvin and I are going as friends, Jodie," she answered impatiently. She thought about how ridiculous the question was. She couldn't imagine herself even *kissing* Colvin!

Jodie sighed and mused, "Christopher and Nicole are pretty much in love, aren't they."

Joanna sighed too. "Yep. They are."

"Do you think—"

Joanna's eyes darted to her sister. "How do you know they haven't already?"

That comment must have caught Jodie off-guard, as her whole expression of wonder fell to shock. The moment was silent, except for the sound of the radio coming from their younger brother Nick's room down the hall.

After a long pause, Jodie turned her head and whispered, "Have they?"

"I didn't say that," Joanna responded. "I just asked what makes you so sure they haven't yet."

"I guess I never thought about it...."

"Oh, Jodie," Joanna sighed again and rested her head on her sister's shoulder.

"Well, now this is going to bother me!" Jodie sprang to her feet, and Joanna fell sideways on the bed. "If Christopher's already done it, don't tell me. I want to believe he's still good."

Now Joanna shot up. "If Christopher's already done it, that's none of our business! And he *is* a very good man!" she added, defending their brother. "Don't you ever hold it against him for falling in love!"

"But it's wrong!" Jodie cried. "It's wrong to have sex without being married!"

Joanna looked down at the floor. "Yes, I know," she uttered softly, shaking her head. The truth of it was that Joanna secretly had the same concerns as Jodie: Christopher was her hero, and she didn't want him to make any mistakes. She thought back to Hawaii when Nicole confided in her that she and Christopher were contemplating having sex. Even though they didn't, Joanna knew that the subject was on their minds.

Joanna wished she could share this with her sister; however, she had promised Nicole that their conversation would remain in confidence. And, while Joanna and Jodie were reasonably close, Joanna's twinship with Christopher superseded all other familial relationships. Joanna was most loyal to her twin brother, and in this instance, the minor age gap of two years forced Joanna to keep a slight distance from her sister.

"Will you be with him the whole night?" Jodie asked. "Can't you watch him to make sure he doesn't sin?"

"Jodie, would you get real?" Joanna cried. "You sound like one of Mom's kindergartners! I am not Christopher's babysitter! He's eighteen years old. He's going to make his own decisions." Now Joanna was irritated, mostly because she didn't want to admit to being equally apprehensive about these same things.

Both girls sat quietly for a few minutes, and tears came to Joanna's eyes. She tried to analyze where all these emotions were coming from. Christopher was growing up faster than she was. Nicole would soon be more important to him than his twin sister, if she wasn't already. Joanna missed the good things about Nathan Hooks. Nathan would be at Prom with someone else. Matthew was taking boring Laura Vigent to the dance, and Laura would be in all the pictures with him as if they were a couple.

That might have been the problem: Laura Vigent. Joanna knew she had no right to be bitter about Matthew taking Laura to Prom, yet now... Well, whether she had a right to be bitter about it or not, she *was* bitter about it.

And Joanna would be with Colvin, who was a nice guy, but... well, if all these people were just pairing up as friends, why couldn't *she* pair up with Matthew?!

"I've got to figure out what to do with my hair," Joanna said suddenly, jumping up. "Could you go get that magazine with all the hairstyles in it? Lisa and Phebe will be here any minute."

As soon as Jodie was out of the room, Joanna allowed a few tears to fall. She was glad she hadn't done her make-up yet, and now she just had to keep her eyes from getting puffy. She sat back down on her bed.

A moment later, Christopher, looking extremely handsome in his suit, sauntered into her room and leaned against the doorway, his hands shoved casually in his pockets. "Well, how is my fashionable designer-dress sister comin' along?" His voice was deep, trying to sound manly and grown-up. Then he stood up straight, walked over and sat next to her on the bed. "What's the matter?"

"Oh, nothing," Joanna groaned. She blew her nose and tossed the Kleenex onto the floor. "Jodie was just in here and she got me thinking about Nathan."

Christopher put his arm compassionately around her.

"I can't help it, Big Brother," Joanna mused sadly. "I can't help thinking that this is so wrong. Nathan and I should have been going to Prom together.

Colvin's great, but Prom is supposed to be romantic, and... and wonderful, and for people that are in love."

"Were you really in *love* with Nathan?" Christopher challenged her gently.

Joanna thought for a moment, unprepared for that response. "Well, I don't know. I loved when he was so sweet to me. I loved Hawaii."

There was a short silence, and then Christopher said, "I think you were in love with the fantasy, or the idea of what *might* lie ahead. But you know in your heart Nathan wasn't the right one for you." Christopher didn't have to remind his sister of how much Nathan liked to drink, even though he was underage. And he didn't have to remind her that this always scared her, being the rule-follower that she was. He didn't have to remind her of any of this, because their twinship radar had them both thinking about all these things without any words. At eighteen, and as immature as he still could be at times, Christopher really was wise and insightful. At least he seemed to be, whenever Joanna needed perspective.

And right now, Joanna needed perspective. She knew her brother was right, although that didn't make her miss having a boyfriend any less. "I guess I see you and Nicole, going so strong, and I just wish our thing didn't have to have fallen apart," she sighed, leaning her head on her brother's shoulder. She thought about the few double-dates she and Nathan had gone on with Christopher and Nicole. Those were some fun times.

Christopher was still, but then lowered his voice and said quietly, "Well... I'm not so sure that we'll be 'going so strong' much longer, Jo-Jo."

Joanna sat up straighter and looked at him. "What do you mean?"

Christopher sighed. "It's complicated, Jo-Jo." Jodie's footsteps pounded up the stairs, so he said, "Well, I'd love to sit here and wallow in depression with you—"

"I am not depressed!" Joanna told him defensively.

Christopher knew that, and he chuckled. "Well, it almost got you to smile! But seriously, everyone is going to be here in a little while for pictures, so you'd better dry up!"

Jodie came back with the magazine, and she positioned the desk chair in front of the mirror. Lisa and Phebe arrived then, and Jodie got right to work on their hair.

Chapter 20: Senior Prom

"Okay, smile, everyone!" Mrs. Conors called enthusiastically, holding her camera. Matthew's mother and Phebe's mother were there as well, snapping pictures of their beautiful children. The group of ten was all coupled up: Christopher and Nicole, Colvin and Joanna, Matthew and Laura, Blake and Lisa, and Aaron and Phebe. The warm weather blessed the Conors' garden wall down near the large pond that bordered the back of their property, hosting a perfect photo site.

When they finished taking pictures, the group hung around for a while eating hors d'oeuvres. It would be too risky to grill out or have a potentially messy meal in their fancy clothing, and it was impossible to get a reservation at one of the only two nice restaurants in town, so the cute little finger foods that the moms had put together would have to sustain them for the evening.

Mrs. Conors offered Nicole a pickle wrapped in a slice of ham, held together by a toothpick, and Joanna watched as the two conversed and laughed like old friends. Nicole got along so well with their family; Joanna was always thankful Christopher had a decent girlfriend.

She also thought about Nathan.

Again.

Nathan had fit right in with her family too, during the few encounters he'd had with them. He would make intelligent conversation with her parents, he and Christopher got along, and he was funny and playful with Nick. He was nice to Jodie and treated her like a friend.

But that's why the people in the popular crowd were popular. They have charisma. They are charming, and they converse well with everyone. Everyone likes them. Nathan had charisma, and Nathan was charming. And everyone liked Nathan.

And then that darn alcohol had to ruin everything! *Stop dwelling on Nathan!* Joanna silently scolded herself.

***

Prom was a tough night for Joanna nonetheless, no matter how much she kept telling herself to let go of these feelings. It seemed as if every time she turned around, she saw Nathan Hooks and his new Prom date: Pelin Yilmaz, of all people! Nathan seemed to be having the time of his life. *How can he not miss me?* Joanna asked herself. Her mind was a million miles away from her friends at this moment. *I was the one who broke things off, so he should miss me! Doesn't he realize what he threw away by his drinking?* And seeing him with Pelin Yilmaz was just salt in the wound. Pelin, the loud, partying, wild-child captain of the pom squad, who had always intimidated Joanna!

Of course, Joanna realized. *That's why he doesn't miss me.*

And there were the slow songs. Feeling nothing for her date, Joanna found the "couples" songs painfully awkward. She sat out for those.

Then *Love Apparition* – a current popular slow song about the love between two friends who are wondering about crossing that line – came on, and Matthew asked Joanna to dance.

"So, what's wrong?" he asked her when they got under the dark lights and away from their group. Joanna didn't respond right away, so Matthew continued. "You're making Colvin nervous. He knows something's bothering you, but he doesn't know what, and he feels like you're not having any fun because you're with him."

"Oh no," Joanna moaned, feeling awful. "Today has just been the longest day, Matthew. It's not Colvin at all. It's... well, I think you know."

"Nathan." Matthew had his arms around her waist, and he pulled her into a hug as they swayed in the darkness.

"I keep seeing him," Joanna said sadly. "I miss him."

"Do you really?" Matthew asked her skeptically. Like Christopher earlier, he hesitated to remind her that she was the one who had called off the relationship.

Joanna looked up at him. "I know he was a jerk when he was drinking, but I also know how sweet he was when he wasn't drinking! And I can't help thinking that maybe he could be like that again! I don't miss the drunk-Nathan, I miss the Nathan from Hawaii."

"But that *is* Nathan, Joanna," Matthew told gently. "Drunk-Nathan *is* Nathan."

But that is Nathan, ***Joanna.*** The tender emphasis in the use of her name sparked yet another set of emotions through her soul.

They continued to sway to the music until the song was over. The strong feelings of not wanting this dance to end caught Joanna by surprise! She felt so safe and secure with Matthew....

But the song did end, and they returned to their table. Joanna tried to give Colvin the attention he deserved, though she still remained preoccupied. She watched her brother and Nicole dance; they looked like they were so in love, and that made her sad, but only for selfish reasons. She was really happy for them, and she just wished she herself could feel like that too.

Are they really in love? she wondered, as more teasing thoughts crept inside her head. She seemed to be spending a lot of energy silently contemplating everything on this night, but she let her thoughts ramble on anyway. She was feeling more selfish lately than she had felt in a very long time. *What did Christopher mean earlier today, when he said something about them maybe not going so strong much longer?*

Midnight bowling was next on the agenda. Showing up at the local bowling alley in their Prom clothes was a memory of its own, but it was more than their attire that was stuck in Joanna's mind. She watched as Laura sat playfully on Matthew's lap, as they laughed and goofed around together. *Laura looks so fake, so wrong for him,* she ruminated bitterly, unable to suppress the snarky thoughts from seeping through her brain. *He doesn't really like her 'like that,'* she told herself. This was true. She knew this for a fact, because she knew Matthew almost better than she knew herself.

So, then Joanna was left with the question of why she was so bothered now by Laura. Matthew had gone out on dates with other girls before! Joanna always gave him advice, and she was never bothered by his interactions with other girls in the past. Yet it annoyed her now to see him treating his date like a queen! Knowing these feelings were selfish made them even harder to process. One of the things Joanna loved about Matthew was that he was such a perfect gentleman, and he always made those around him feel special and important. Matthew was doing the right thing by making sure his date had a great time at their prom, while Joanna sat there wallowing in her own misery, practically ignoring Colvin, the nice guy who agreed to go with her so that they all could be part of the group. She felt even more terrible after that!

As Joanna retreated to a bench near the score table, Phebe came over and sat next to her. She scooped the poof of her rose-colored gown over to one side and said, "Whew! I can't believe I have the high score this far into the game!"

"Well, three strikes in a row helped," Joanna reminded her.

"Oh, and get this. Aaron whispered to me that I'm the prettiest girl here!"

Joanna rolled her eyes and mentally reclassified her best friend to the category of 'annoying,' even though Joanna appreciated the diversion from thinking about what a lame date she herself was being for Colvin. But Joanna was still feeling crabby. She was tired, and emotional, and it didn't take long for her to max out on Phebe being annoying. Phebe was wonderful, and she and Joanna had been best friends pretty much since kindergarten, but comments like this were just plain annoying. Sometimes, Phebe would get so full of herself that Joanna would have to put her in her place. To Phebe's statement about Aaron saying she was the prettiest girl in the group, Joanna said, "Well, of course he's going to say that, Phebe. He's being a good date. It's not like he's going to go up to you and say that *Lisa's* the prettiest girl in the group."

Not allowing Joanna to take away her compliment, Phebe retorted, "Well, he didn't have to say anything at all! But he did, so he must mean it."

"Okay."

"He seems in awe of me," Phebe went on thoughtfully, resting her elbows on her knees and gazing up at the scoreboard. "He keeps staring at me. I wonder if he likes me *like that.*"

At this point, Joanna didn't really care whether Aaron Mickels liked Phebe *like that*, so she said, "Everyone seems to be having a good time tonight." It was a challenge to hide how crabby she was feeling!

"You're kind of aloof tonight, Jay. *I* think *you* look nice, even if Colvin isn't gushing over *you.*"

Joanna leaned forward and put her face in her hands. "I am so tired! How late are we going to be here tonight? I'm ready to be done!"

Lisa came over then, sat down next to Joanna, and told Phebe it was her turn to bowl. Joanna looked up and saw Laura laughing shyly about the gutter ball she had just rolled. Matthew patted her sympathetically on the shoulder.

Even though Lisa and Phebe were both Joanna's best friend, Joanna could max out on Phebe under certain conditions. Lisa never reached the degree of annoying that Phebe sometimes peaked at, so Joanna said to Lisa, "Is she even having fun?"

"Who? Phebe?" Lisa asked as she dug into her little purse for her lip gloss.

"Laura," Joanna snapped.

Lisa looked over to where the others were standing and said, "Laura? Yeah, I think so. Why?"

Joanna sat back and adjusted her dress as she crossed her legs, showing off her left blue and red bowling shoe underneath. "I don't know. She looks so uncomfortable. Or out of place, maybe."

Lisa looked over there again. "Hmmm. I don't know. She seems to be having a good time. She's friendly and conversational. A little more so than at lunch!"

"Oh. Okay. Well, good," Joanna said, even though she didn't mean *good* at all. She was hoping that Laura was *not* having a good time, and that it would be more obvious. Or, to be perfectly and selfishly honest, she hoped that *Matthew* was not having a good time, with Laura as his date. "I just didn't know how it'd go since she's kind of new to our group," Joanna concluded.

"I think she's doing fine. She's sweet. I don't think she ever would have had the confidence to go to Prom if you hadn't helped set that up with Matthew for her," Lisa said kindly. Lisa was always so kind.

The night dragged on, but eventually, everyone went home.

Why do I even care that Matthew took Laura to Prom? I didn't want him to take me, remember? I didn't want him to take me because then everyone would think he liked me or that I liked him. We have a *Freundschaft*, and that's all it is! He didn't even really want to go, remember? I'M the one who told him to ask Laura, because I knew she kind of liked him! I set this all up, and now I'm complaining about it! ☹

Chapter 21: Heart to Heart

It was not until Sunday that Joanna got to talk to her brother, heart to heart. Joanna trusted Christopher with some of her deep thoughts, and he never betrayed that trust. There were times when he thought she was a little wacky, or he didn't understand the girl drama behind things, but in the end, he always respected her and maintained the honest relationship they had with each other. Late in the warm afternoon that day, Joanna sat out in their garden near the pond, writing in her journal.

The small terrace at the water's edge, with its brick stone surface and six-foot trellis along the east side, was a quiet place that Joanna often retreated to when she wanted to write. Her grandfather had crafted the two wooden benches and little table that stood in the corner near the elevated flower beds; the whole set up was quite serene.

After only a half-page of journaling, she could hear her brother's footsteps as he padded his way down the lawn.

"Hey," Christopher said. He sat on the bench opposite her.

"Hey."

"You writin' more of your deepest, darkest secrets?"

Joanna turned toward her brother and closed her book. "Christopher, if I tell you something, do you promise never to tell a soul, or think I'm weird, or distort it in any way? Will you just help me figure this out?"

Christopher nodded, and waited for her to continue. He had come out there to talk to her, to sort out some of his own emotions, but he saw that he was needed for advice first.

Joanna took a deep breath. "I think I like Matthew."

Silence. Only the sounds of a squawking goose in the distance, and a few birds chirping in the trees, hung over them.

"Did you hear me?" Joanna asked him. "I said I think I *like* Matthew. Matthew Carmichael. Our *friend.*"

Finally, her brother asked calmly, "Why do you think this?"

"I don't know! It's like, suddenly this weekend, at Prom and everything, all these weird, strange feelings are running loose inside of me whenever I'm around him. Like when he and I danced together, I think that was the best dance of my life! And it's basically the only one I remember from last night." She paused, but then went on. "And Laura just looks so wrong with him."

Christopher almost choked a laugh. "Jo-Jo, *you* were the one who invited her into our group! I thought you were friends with her! Aren't you the one who set them up for Prom?"

"I *know!*" she exclaimed in frustration. "I *know* that, Big Brother. I thought it would be okay."

"Well, you really should have minded your own business. He didn't even want to go, and suddenly he felt all obligated because you asked him to take her, and he felt sorry for her..."

Joanna lit up for a moment. "Really? He didn't want to go?"

"Jo-Jo, c'mon." Clearly, Christopher was not in the mood for his sister to pretend to be naïve about all this.

"Well, it seemed like a good idea at the time," Joanna pouted, turning to look back out at the pond. "But then I realized... I don't know. She's so awkward. And I feel so close to Matthew. I'm just confused, I guess."

"You are close to Matthew," Christopher reminded her. "You're his best friend."

"No, I'm not. You are," Joanna said.

"I'm his best guy friend," said Christopher. "And for going out and doing stuff, I'm his bro. But I seriously think he feels closer to you when it comes to the deep stuff... You know what I mean? He comes to me when he's got a typical problem, like when he scraped the car, or when he forgot his wallet that one time and was headed out on a date after school. But if he's seriously got a problem, about girls or things that require understanding, think about it. He always goes to you first."

The idea of Matthew actually being drawn to her scared Joanna, so she tried to deny it. "You're understanding," she told her brother.

Christopher disagreed. "Not the way I should be with him. To me, it's like, man-up and figure it out! But you provide him with the support he needs, and you allow him to break down a little bit when he has to get away from putting up a strong front. You know what I mean?"

Joanna just nodded. The vulnerability she felt now was unsettling.

"So, I guess we're both his best friend, but really, I've never seen Matthew cry. But I bet you have."

Joanna thought for a moment, and then nodded again. "Yeah, yes, I have. How'd you know?"

Christopher shrugged his shoulders. "Guys aren't allowed to cry, but we all have to at one time or another. And I know when they had to put Rex down last year, he was heartbroken. But he'd never show it, not even to me. Even though I knew probably better than anyone how much that dog meant to him, and I'd never laugh at him, still."

"But Matthew is such a good friend to me, too, you know?" Joanna said. "He was there for me when I broke up with Nathan—"

"Hey!" Christopher jumped in defensively, "I warned you Nathan was a partier!"

"I know!" moaned Joanna impatiently, "but you were, like, kind of annoying about it. Like, *I told you so. He's a drinker, you're not going to like it!* Matthew was more like, *Dang, what happened to Hawaii?.*" Her brother looked a little hurt, so Joanna leaned over and punched his arm, and went on, "Christopher, I really liked Nathan. It was very hard for me to dump him. You only saw the one bad thing about him, therefore it was very simple to you: Drop him. But Matthew understood how great Hawaii was, and understood that I didn't want to give that up. The way you acted made me want to stay with him, just to spite you!"

"Joanna, Nathan hit you. If you let that go once, regardless of whether he was drunk or not, you're screwed for the rest of your life! Was I the only one who saw this?" Christopher planned to go into law enforcement after college, so he was always on it when it came to protecting his favorite people.

"That's not the point! Yes, you were right, but that doesn't mean that was the best way to go about it. And anyway, that isn't the issue we're discussing here. I'm confused about Matthew. Do I like him as more than a friend or not?"

Christopher tried to ignore his bruised ego to give this some thought. "I don't think you like Matthew like that. Can you see yourself kissing him? Making out with him?"

Joanna did not answer right away. She liked hugging him... but making out with him? She wasn't so sure about that...

"Are you attracted to him?" Christopher went on. "Do you want him to *want* you? To desire you? Do you want him looking lustfully into your eyes? Do you want him undressing you..."

"Christopher, STOP!" she cried, giggling but feeling dirty at the same time.

"I think," he finished up, "that you are not in love with him, but you are in love with his friendship."

Freundschaft.

"He truly cares about you as a friend," Christopher went on. "And that is really comforting to know. That's why you two make such good friends. But do you really think you could share one life together? I mean, I guess you like snowmobiles and four-wheelers and all that stuff we do, but... well, if you guys had a date planned for Saturday night, who would he ask for ideas on what to do? Where would he get all of his advice from? You don't want him askin' *me* if it's too soon for him to put his hand up your shirt, do ya?"

"Christopher, stop it!" Joanna cried, giggling again. "You're making me feel all gross!"

Christopher laughed. "I'm just kidding. But am I making sense?"

"Yes. Thank you. ...OHHH!" she laughed now too. "I can't believe you said that!" She whacked his arm.

"Well, it's true, isn't it? Doesn't Matthew always ask you first before he takes the next step with a girl?"

Joanna smiled. "Once. He did *once*. But that's because he's shy. He didn't want to do anything wrong."

"I know. And you could never stand his shyness!" Christopher told her. "You guys would never be able to do anything because he'd be so afraid of offending you!"

"You're right," Joanna nodded. Now her mind was racing with things she hadn't considered, so she changed the subject. "So, did *you* have fun at Prom?"

Christopher smiled. "Yes, I did. It was pretty fun."

"Jodie is worried about you, you know."

"Why?"

After Tomorrow

Joanna chuckled a nervous-chuckle. "She is worried about you having sex with Nicole."

"What?!"

"She was worried that you would do it because it was Prom night." Joanna didn't want to pressure her brother into saying whether he had or hadn't; however, her curiosity was killing her, and she wanted him to know that if he chose to tell her, she would not judge him.

Christopher lowered his voice. "Well, just between you and me—"

"Did you?" Joanna couldn't help jumping in.

"No."

Joanna subtly breathed a sigh of relief.

"We talked about it. We've talked about it a lot, actually," Christopher went on, chuckling a little to himself. "But you know, I mentioned to you yesterday that I'm not really sure where this is going. And for the first time... We don't want to do it just anywhere. Where would we have done it anyway? We were with you guys pretty much the whole night!"

Joanna nodded.

"Nicole wants to wait until she's married," he finished up.

"That's good, right? Isn't that what you want? Aren't you willing to wait?" Joanna asked him.

"For her? That's the thing. When she told me that, it kinda scared me, Jo-Jo, because I don't know that I want to *marry* her. I love her, but... Man, I don't want to think about marriage for a long time. I..." He paused, and then said, "Aw crap, Jo-Jo, don't repeat this, okay? I've got some crap to figure out too, so please don't say anything to anyone." Christopher knew he didn't need to wait for the promise; he could trust his twin sister for all the same reasons he had just explained about Matthew trusting her.

He went on. "We're graduating soon. We're moving on to college in the fall. She's goin' off to Montana... She wants to do the long-distance thing but... Oh, Jo-Jo. I feel like such a jerk saying this, but... I kinda want to see what else is out there, you know? I mean, I love Nicole. She's great! But I don't want this type of permanency yet."

Joanna nodded.

"I mean," Christopher went on, hoping to verbalize his thought process in a way that made sense, "I've had a wonderful year with Nicole. Our relationship was perfect for this time of my life. But I'm heading into a new life now, and she's going to be fourteen hours away. I don't know how we'd hang onto that. And she wants to be a doctor. That's a very lofty goal and it's very respectable, but I don't know if I want to be married to a doctor. It's just... Yeah. I feel terrible about it, but I just don't want to continue this." After a pause, he justified, "I always thought of her as my 'high school girlfriend,' but I've never really thought of her as my 'forever.'"

Joanna nodded again, and thought about how to respond. Her brother already had clarity; what he needed from her was validation that it was okay to feel this way. "Sounds like you know what you want," she said finally. "Have you told her any of this?"

Christopher shook his head. "I've been avoiding it. I don't want to hurt her. I was sort of hoping she'd come to this conclusion herself and want to be done with me!"

Now Joanna shook her head. "Girls don't think that way, Big Brother. Going away to college – especially somewhere that is more than a long car ride away like Montana – is pretty scary. She's going to want to have that security of you to hold onto when she heads into this new chapter of life. You'd better tell her soon if you're seriously going to break it off. DON'T wait until the end of the summer!" she warned.

Joanna was pretty wise and insightful herself. It was a lot easier to be wise and insightful about someone else's situation than it was for her own.

Christopher didn't say anything, but he thought about his sister's advice. Joanna went on, "If you drag this on through the summer, she's going to change her mind about waiting until she gets married to have sex. She's going to want to do it with you because it will be so dramatic and meaningful before the big change, and if you have sex with her, she will *really* want to hang onto you throughout college. And she'll believe that you will too, because in a girl's mind, if you have sex with her, you're in it for the long haul."

Christopher nodded. "Yeah, yeah, you're right Jo-Jo. You are right."

After another quiet moment, Joanna lightened things up a little. "Aaron asked me the other night if you guys have done it yet," she said. "I told him I didn't know. I sort of led him to believe you have, since he talks like he's such a sex fiend himself."

"You did?"

"Well, it's none of his business, Christopher. If you guys did do it, nobody should know except you and Nicole. And me. Just kidding," she added.

"I'd probably tell you," Christopher said. "Only because I couldn't not tell *you*. Aaron? Pfff! He's a tool; I don't care what he thinks. But Jodie! She shouldn't be thinking about this. She's the last person I'd tell; she'd have me rotting in hell before I'd have a chance to finish my sentence! I don't even know that I'd tell Matthew."

Joanna looked out at the water then, and smiled to herself. She wondered how she ever got so lucky.

***

Joanna's journal continued to be a place of refuge for her. What had started out as a random gift now became a safe place where she could sort out feelings, or make strong judgments about people and things that she would never want to say aloud. After her talk with Christopher, she really needed her journal to organize her thoughts, although she didn't really come to any conclusions.

I think I like Matthew, Herr Journal. As more than a friend, I mean. He is so caring, and kind, and he's such a good person. I talked to Christopher about this, and he thinks I'm confusing strong feelings about our *Freundschaft* with romantic feelings. He asked me if I could imagine myself kissing Matthew. I told him ew, that's gross, but the truth is, I think I would like it if Matthew kissed me!!

But I don't EVER want to lose our close friendship, so I can't let on about any of this until I figure it out. I thought I missed Nathan... but Christopher is right: I miss the fantasy of what *might have been* with Nathan. Maybe I don't like Matthew like that at all, I just want someone who's not a loser and who doesn't do things like drink and throw things. I don't really know. ughh.

Chapter 22: Follow Up with Phebe

That evening, Joanna met Phebe down by the river on her bike. "Aaron called me today. He wants to go out again!" Phebe exclaimed right away.

"Oh? That's great! Do you want to go out with him again? What are you guys going to do?"

"We're going to Dream Belle's after school tomorrow," Phebe answered. "We are going to work on our Spanish assignment together there, too, because there's one last assignment that's due Tuesday, and we didn't want to work on it over Prom weekend."

"Okay. So..." Joanna was confused; she tried to think of how she wanted to phrase her question, but ended up just being straight up. "What *is* the deal with you two? Weren't you 'going out' when we were in Hawaii?"

Phebe sighed and rolled her eyes. "Yes, I guess, sort of. I don't know, Jay. Let's not worry about that. Let's just talk about what we're doing right *now*."

The girls chained up their bikes and started to walk along the trail down by the water. A lot of people were out. Although there had been talk of putting a bike lane alongside the pedestrian trail so that cyclists could hustle along the river on their own path, construction hadn't started yet. It seemed like there were a lot of cyclists out today.

Joanna's mind started to wander. *I wonder if Matthew called Laura today. Colvin hasn't called me, but I would never expect him to. I should probably call him and apologize for being such a lame date!*

"...He said he is super tired today, but he said it was worth it," Phebe went on. "We didn't get home until like two-thirty."

"Two-thirty!" Joanna cried. She was good at keeping up with conversations, even while daydreaming. "What in the world were you doing until two-thirty?!" She and Christopher had both gotten home from Prom just after one-o'clock.

Phebe smiled and said devilishly, "Wouldn't *you* like to know!"

"Phebe, shut up. What'd you do? Go out to Midpoint?"

"*Maaaybe...*"

The large gravel parking lot just at the south end of town, known as the Midpoint Make-Out Lot, got its name from its location being half-way between the city limits of Woodland Hills and the city limits of the neighboring community, Cannon Valley. There was a trailhead at the parking lot, for a trail that ran alongside the country road, connecting the two towns. Because Cannon Valley had so many hiking trails and waterfalls, people often came there from surrounding areas to hike and experience the beautiful outdoors in the country. The parking lot was known as a popular make-out spot for locals, however, at night when the tourists were gone.

Joanna just rolled her eyes.

"He kissed me when we first got to the car!" Phebe justified, while giggling. "At the bowling alley, when we were done, he kissed me and said we shouldn't waste this beautiful night sky. Isn't that romantic? *Let's not waste this beautiful night sky.* He said, *The stars match your eyes...*"

Joanna rolled her eyes again. "*Let's not waste this beautiful night sky, because I still want to get in your pants. Hey! I know! Let's go park at Midpoint!*"

Phebe giggled, clearly not ashamed of anything she might have done the night before with her prom date. "Well, let's just say we did a few things that were new to me," she said, still smiling. But then she quickly added, "Not *that*-that. But still. And he's a *great* kisser, by the way."

"Two-thirty?" Joanna repeated, still unable to believe her friend was out that late. "Were your parents up when you got home?"

"My mom was asleep on the couch. I woke her when I got home, told her we were bowling and all that. It was fine."

Joanna's mind started to wander again. *I wonder what time Matthew got home. There is NO WAY he'd take Laura to a make-out spot!*

Always looking for gossip, Phebe mused, "Well, what about Christopher?" She tried to sound mysterious. "He and Nicole... Prom night... They've been together for like a year now, haven't they?"

"Yeah... We're not going to talk about my brother," Joanna told her in a tone that was sweet, yet final.

"Okay, then how about you and Colvin? Did he kiss you or anything? Lisa said Blake kissed her out on the dance floor and then later before they got to the bowling alley!"

"Well, I had absolutely no desire for Colvin to kiss me. And frankly, the thought of it sort of repulses me, so thank you very much for that visual."

"Joanna!"

"Well seriously, Phebe! I mean, I like the dude and all, he's a nice guy, but everything doesn't have to turn into romance and kissing and all that, does it?"

"Well, I know that! I'm just saying, it was *Prom*, and everything was romantic, so a little kiss is nice! Lisa's not like *in love* with Blake now or anything, and she still let him kiss her. It's the right thing to do under those circumstances."

"Fine," Joanna replied shortly.

"Sheesh!" Phebe complained. "You were crabby last night and now you're all crabby again."

"Well!" Joanna huffed. "I just don't think these are things that ought to be made public!"

"A *kiss*? Who cares that she told me he gave her a kiss! That's not private! It's —"

"Oh, never mind. Never mind!"

"Well, really!"

"I'm sorry," Joanna apologized then. "I'm sorry, Pheebs. I'm just... Prom was just bad timing this year. I'm annoyed that Nathan was there with *Pelin*, and I am annoyed at myself for being a dud with Colvin. And I just think that we're getting to be adults now and we probably shouldn't be sharing every intimate detail with each other about some of these things. Because then if word gets out, for example, about Blake kissing Lisa, or whatever, then you know how that whole thing goes! The whole school will be after her: *Oh! Are you guys going out now? Blah blah blah!*"

"Yeah, yeah, yeah, whatever. Nathan doesn't even like Pelin anyway," Phebe told her, realizing that the real issue behind Joanna's grumpiness was her ex-boyfriend bringing the gorgeous Turkish hot-body, Pelin Yilmaz, to Prom. "He just asked her because she's the only girl in our class who is at least half as pretty as you, and once he dated you, he can't go down."

"That's not true," Joanna said sadly. She *knew* that wasn't true. Nathan dating Joanna was a step down for him, so of course he would go back to the popular crowd.

However, this idea that Phebe presented did make Joanna feel a little better!

And Phebe swore it was true. "Aaron told me this at Prom!" she attested. "Blake made a comment like, *Wow, it didn't take Hooks very long to move on!* And then Aaron said that Nathan said that he – Nathan – *had* to go to Prom this year, and he *had* to find someone better looking than JC or else he wouldn't go, and evidently all the guys agreed that Pelin was his only choice if that was his criteria."

All Joanna could say to that was, "Hmmm."

Phebe gave me an explanation today for how Nathan ended up taking Pelin to Prom. I'm not sure it's 100% accurate, but Phebe is usually privy to this kind of information, so it's certainly possible. And it's the only story anyone has about this at this point anyway, so I'll take it! ☺

Chapter 23: Luke

During the latter weeks of the spring, Luke Mason began paying more and more attention to Joanna when they worked together at the Toy Store. He seemed to find Joanna intriguing, and he often pursued conversation with her as if only to see how she would respond. She was more receptive to him than she was to Mike Grenzesky, and that was a victory Luke embraced. And while he surely knew she was way out of his league, he playfully pestered her at work anyway.

Joanna admitted to herself that she liked the attention, though she wasn't sure yet if she felt anything for Luke. Lately she started to look forward to shifts with him. His attention was different than the attention she occasionally received from other guys. Luke was immature. Luke was even a little bit of a loser, sort of, but something about his attention made Joanna feel sexy. Joanna knew in her head that attention from Luke was nothing to be proud of, but even so, she liked how it made her *feel*. *She* knew that Luke knew she was out of his league, but that made her feel cool.

Friday night at work that week was typical for the Toy Store crew. Luke bought a bag of Gummi Worms, which he left for Joanna at the Customer Service desk. Joanna loved Gummi Worms. At one point, Luke came up there to empty the returned merchandise bin, and since no one else was around, he took one of the worms and stepped up close to Joanna. "Yo."

Her eyes caught his, gray and hidden behind his glasses. "Yo."

He quickly dropped the Gummi Worm down the front of her shirt.

Pretending to be shocked, Joanna looked around to be sure no one saw as she retrieved the worm. Before handing it back to him, she flicked it around as she spoke. "I believe this is yours?"

Luke ate it with a big smile, but then complained of the perfumy taste on it. Joanna rolled her eyes and walked away. She was always rolling her eyes at Luke's dumb, immature antics.

Later as she walked back to the break room, Luke came up behind her and pulled on her bra strap, which was a concentrated effort, given that she had a thick fabric smock on over her cotton shirt.

After Tomorrow

While most of Luke's childish behaviors made Joanna simply roll her eyes and giggle, this one was not okay. She whipped around and glared at him. He was about two inches shorter than her, which she knew was intimidating to him, yet exciting at the same time.

"What are we, in Junior High?" she demanded coolly, and her tone was serious. Her bright eyes pierced him. "DON'T ever do *that* again."

"Ohhh!" he said, stepping back but continuing to walk. He put his hands up innocently while vocalizing a note to himself: "Don't touch the undergarments."

That night, when Joanna was home and in bed, her big, poofy tomcat crawled on top of her stomach as she lay there thinking about her night at work. Black-Cat-Black, jokingly named because of his patchy coat when Joanna rescued him from Matthew's grandparents' farm ten years earlier, was gentle and cuddly. Joanna stroked her cat's silky fur while thinking about Luke. She realized she had been thinking a lot about Luke lately. Maybe it was because she had worked almost every night that week, and so had he. Maybe it was because she was done over-analyzing the breakup with Nathan, and she needed to feel sexy again. Maybe it was because Luke was so weird, and the challenge to figure him out was kind of exciting. Maybe it was because he was so insecure, and she felt bad that he didn't seem to like himself. Maybe it was because his teddy-bear body was comfortable – and hot! – to her. Maybe it was because she knew Luke found her to be hot, and she liked that. Maybe it was because he was sooooooo different from Nathan and any other guy she might be matched up with. Maybe it was because he was not a match to her at all – he couldn't be more opposite!

Maybe it was because she knew that her co-worker, Dulcie Brinkman, had the hots for Luke, but Luke couldn't stand Dulcie.

Joanna scratched behind Black-Cat-Black's ears, and his purr grew louder.

Dulcie Brinkman was a girl that worked at the Toy Store who was the same age as Joanna, but Dulcie went to Middleton, the other high school in the area. Dulcie would be more of a match for Luke; she was headed to community college, maybe, though she was unsure of what she wanted to do with her life. She was loud and overbearing, to the point of being annoying to most who knew her. She was overconfident and borderline obnoxious, and from what Joanna could tell, she desired to be a superstar in this part-time job. She viewed the Customer Service Area as the highest position in the store, even though that was far from true. She wanted to work in the

Service Area every chance she got, but usually management preferred to have Joanna up there. While Dulcie could perform the basic tasks well, which made her look good on paper, she was so incredibly *annoying* that the management often tried to hide her in other areas of the store so as not to compromise their operations.

There were many reasons to explain why so much of Luke seemed to be in Joanna's head, but none were more persistent than the one she didn't want to admit to: She was suppressing her feelings for Matthew, and she was replacing them with what might be feelings for Luke.

As Joanna lay in bed that night, she remembered some of Luke's other antics that week. He had told her he was a virgin – probably to see what her reaction would be and whether she would even believe him.

"I am!" he had insisted, as they straightened the Barbie aisle together earlier in the week. "I haven't had sex with anyone, ever."

"You're such a liar," Joanna grumbled, as she crouched down to pull two Skipper dolls out from behind a row of Wedding Barbies. The idea of this guy still being a virgin at his age was intriguing to her, but she knew it couldn't be true.

"Why don't you believe that I am a virgin?" he asked her.

Joanna stood up. "Luke," she said pointedly, "you are twenty-three years old, and frankly, you don't strike me as one who is very... let's just say, *values-oriented*. So, I am quite sure you are not *saving yourself* for marriage."

Luke laughed and said, "Well, I'm still a virgin, but not by choice. I'm telling you: Girls don't like me."

Joanna set the two Skipper dolls in their proper location on a different shelf and said, "*That's* not true, either."

Yes, Luke was interesting to say the least.

Joanna then thought about that next morning, after that night at work. Matthew had come up to Joanna at her locker at school. "Hey," he'd said, as she spun the dial of the combination lock around a few times.

"Hey."

"What was that all about with Luke last night at work?" Matthew had asked her curiously.

Joanna continued spinning the dial with her thumb, but her attempt to unlock it was futile. Her thumb just danced aimlessly around the numbers, with its sparkly neon-blue nail polish glimmering under her shadow. She was completely not-focused and now couldn't even think of which numbers she should be spinning towards on the padlock. "What do you mean?" she responded, not looking up. Matthew had been at the store the night before also.

"You guys were in the Barbie aisle... all that talk about being a virgin?"

Oh. Matthew must have been straightening in a nearby aisle and overheard them.

Joanna had stopped spinning her lock and looked up at him, and then rolled her eyes and shook her head. She pressed her lips together, briefly revealing the dimple in her left cheek. "I don't know. He was trying to convince me he is a virgin."

Matthew had a confused expression on his face, and Joanna just looked at him. *Why is he asking me about this?* she wondered. *Why does Matthew care about the stupid conversations I had with Luke last night?*

As Joanna lay in bed now, she grabbed her journal from under her pillow and scribbled,

Stupid conversations. That's what I have with Luke. He's so immature!

Then she thought about Matthew. Everything with Matthew was so intelligent, so much higher. *But that's boring,* she wrote. And because she herself still had a teeny bit of maturing to do, she added, trying to convince herself: *Matthew is boring. Luke is entertaining!!*

***

"Hey, Dad, what do you think of my new watch?" Joanna asked her father the next day, after she and Jodie had come back from the Mall. Woodland Hills had a busy shopping hub in the center of town that included the Toy Store, and the locals referred to it as "the Mall." Target and Menards were the big draw at this "mall," but there were also several restaurants, a grocery store, and other outlets to accommodate the residents. Tourists shopped at Riverside, the trendy, upscale strip along the river, but the locals mostly shopped at the Mall.

It was Saturday, and Mr. Conors had just entered the kitchen, where the family was gathering for dinner. Joanna held her wrist up to him. Her new Swatch-watch was huge, with giant numbers on it. The whole thing looked clunky, hanging on her skinny wrist.

Mr. Conors took her arm and squinted as he looked at the colorful face of the watch. "I don't know. I can't really see it," he commented.

Joanna moved her arm slightly, wondering if the reflection from the light over the table was hindering his view. "Why can't you see it?" she asked.

"Well, I don't know," he said with a perfectly straight face. "I don't think the numbers are big enough."

Joanna burst out laughing then, finally getting her father's joke.

"What do you need such a big watch for?" her younger brother Nick asked.

"For Germany," Joanna replied, as if that were a silly question. "I'll have to know what *Uhr* it is."

In less than two weeks, Joanna and Christopher would be going to Germany for almost the whole month of June, with others from the German classes at school. It was an exchange program, and they each would be staying with a host family of a same-age student that lived in the small town of Waldheim. Joanna and Christopher, and Udo Meikler, were the only seniors going; everyone else was from other classes, so the twins didn't know them as well. It was going to be quite an adventure, and they were really looking forward to it!

Mrs. Conors was pulling chicken out of the oven, and Jodie was pouring milk into the glasses, when Christopher came home and slumped into a chair at the table. "Well," he sighed, capturing the attention of the entire family. "It's over. It's completely over. I broke up with Nicole."

"What?!" Jodie cried immediately, almost dropping the milk jug.

"Broke up with her?" Nick questioned, wondering what exactly that meant. At ten years old, he hadn't quite figured out the whole concept of a teenage relationship yet. Joanna just looked at her twin, and Mr. Conors was quiet.

"Oh my!" Mrs. Conors exclaimed, setting the chicken down and pulling off her oven mitts. When Christopher didn't respond to anyone's reaction, his mother went on, "That's quite a headline to come home with. How did this all come about?"

✳✳✳

That night in bed, for the second night in a row, Joanna's racing thoughts delayed her sleep. She was proud of her brother for breaking off the relationship that he admitted he had checked out of, and she was glad he didn't drag things on when his heart wasn't in it. But she wondered what this meant for him now. She wondered if her brother would flirt with girls the way Luke flirted with her. She wondered if Christopher would become a player. He had said that he wanted to "see what else is out there."

What exactly does that mean?

It was pretty early to be in bed for a Saturday night when Joanna heard the phone ring. A moment later, Mrs. Conors tapped softly on her door and poked her head in the room. "Are you awake, Sweet Pea? The phone is for you."

It was Luke.

Luke had never called Joanna before!

"Why are you calling me?" Joanna whispered, almost excitedly, as she pulled the cordless phone with her under the covers in her bed. Black-Cat-Black was burrowed next to her.

"Because I'm bored."

"How'd you get my number?"

"I got it from Grenzesky!" Luke replied proudly.

"Mike Grenzesky?" Joanna questioned. "Why would he have my number?"

"He knows everything about you," Luke joked. "That guy is in love with you!"

"Shut up." Black-Cat-Black stretched out alongside Joanna's body, and his purr grew stronger.

Joanna and Luke talked on the phone for a long time – a long time about nothing, really, because there wasn't much depth to Luke. Joanna had depth. Joanna liked depth. Joanna needed depth. There wasn't much depth to Luke, but he was so interesting with his unpredictability that she was drawn to conversation with him nonetheless.

Joanna noticed that Luke seemed to sabotage the good things in his life. It was as if he never trusted that good things could be true for him. He was strange in the way of being inconsistent, and his inconsistency kept Joanna guessing. She knew he was a piece of work, and she was drawn to the challenge of figuring him out.

"I know it bothers you that I'm not in school," he said, since the conversation had already hit a lull.

"Why would I care whether you're in school or not?" she asked him. His comment confused her, but, well, most things about Luke confused her.

"'Cuz you do, and I know it bothers you."

"I don't really care whether you're in school or not, Luke."

"Yes, you do, because I should be doing something with my life and I'm not."

"Well, if you know you should be doing something with your life, why don't you do something with your life?"

"I don't know." His reply was dismissive, and quick.

"Luke, why'd you call me?"

"To see if you'd talk to me. I figured you'd hang up."

"Why would I hang up?"

"Because you wouldn't want to talk to me. Are you pissed that I called you?"

Now things were really going in circles. Luke was difficult. Later after the call ended, Joanna lay in bed and replayed the phone conversation in her head. Yes, it was stupid and empty. Yes, Luke was difficult and weird.

Yet, Joanna looked forward to working with him the next day.

***

Sunday at the Toy Store started out with the annoying Dulcie Brinkman coming up to Joanna as they clocked in together. "Joanna, I want to be in the Service Area today. It's my turn, because you got to be there on Friday night. You can be on the salesfloor and do RGD."

Joanna didn't say anything; she just walked over to the Service Area, where Ken was planning out the schedule. Honestly, Joanna didn't care whether she was up front in Customer Service or out on the salesfloor. Luke would be working that day. If Joanna was on the floor, she'd be able to work with Luke. But clearly, at least in Dulcie's eyes, the Service Area held more prestige. And Joanna wouldn't mind being chosen over Dulcie for that prestige!

"Ken, it's my turn to be in the Service Area today!" Dulcie boldly announced to their manager as she followed Joanna to the counter. Taken a bit by surprise, Ken looked at Joanna. Joanna tried to stifle a little giggle and shrugged. She said quietly to him, "Evidently, we 'take turns' now?" Her eyes were smiling but her words remained neutral.

Ken kept a straight face with smiling eyes as well, and said with authority, "I need Joanna up front to run things today. Dulcie, you can go find Ned to see what he needs you to do out on the floor."

"Awww!" Dulcie stomped her foot and headed out to find the salesfloor supervisor.

"Besides," Ken said off-handedly, looking down at the schedule again and pretending to be talking to himself, "Luke won't get any work done if I have Joanna out there." Then he looked at Joanna to see if she heard him. She smiled and grabbed the register keys from the drawer.

Luke's juvenile attention towards Joanna manifested itself that day in spite of him working in a different area of the store. And even though Joanna knew it was stupid, his antics continued to make her laugh and feel sexy.

The store was busy, and once when Joanna paged Luke over the intercom system to ask him to check something for a customer, he wasn't able to answer her.

Since he had never responded to the page, it was a good excuse for him later to go up to the Customer Service desk to see Joanna. "I was with a customer earlier," he explained. "D'you still want me?"

Joanna looked around to ensure no one was within earshot, and then she said quietly, in a flirty but sarcastic tone, "Yeah, Luke. I still *want* you."

"Do you really?!" he exclaimed, exhilarated.

She sighed dramatically and said in her regular voice, "Well, I did, but you ignored me, so I've moved on." It was fun to flirt with him.

Luke met up with Joanna when she brought a box back to the storeroom. He put his arm around her and said quietly, into her ear, "So, do you really want me?"

Joanna let herself slide comfortably inside his arm, and she raised an eyebrow. "Yeah, Luke, I do."

"Okay, let's do it right here!" he joked, stepping back and pointing to a hidden bay surrounded by boxed merchandise.

"Shut up."

Joanna knew that Luke liked getting a reaction out of her by engaging her through his antics. But occasionally her innocence left her confused, and the confused reaction was even more entertaining. He joked with her as they walked out of the dimly lit storeroom, "You gonna chabe me then?"

She just looked at him. After a moment of thought, she squinted her eyes and said coolly, "I don't know what that means."

Luke burst out laughing and walked away. When Joanna returned to the front end, Christopher came up to give her a 3-ring binder that belonged in the Service Area. Joanna said, "Christopher, what does *chabe me* mean?"

"*Chabe me?*" he repeated in a whisper. He half-chuckled. "Where'd ya hear that?"

"Luke just asked me if I'm going to *chabe* him."

Christopher leaned in and whispered the translation for the slang term in her ear.

Joanna's eyes popped out of her head and she exclaimed, "Christopher Michael!"

Christopher found this to be hilarious and cried, "YOU asked! I'm not the one who said it!"

"Stop!" she screeched. "That's disgusting!"

He leaned up close to her and advised, "Yeah, and you'd better not be doin' any of that with that Luke character, Joanna Marie." He handed her the binder and walked away.

Luke discovered how ticklish Joanna was later that day, when she brought him a case of hair accessories to put away in one of the aisles. Luke came up to her, put his arm around her, and poked his finger into her side. Not wanting to be seen goofing around on the job, Joanna pushed him away just as Matthew happened to be walking by. Matthew stopped, turned toward them down the aisle, and said, "Luke, leave Joanna alone and get back to work. I don't think she appreciates that."

As soon as Matthew left, Luke made a face and muttered a cruel, derogatory remark.

His attack stung Joanna. And *that* crossed the line.

Upon hearing the remark, which included the f-word, she shot him a look. Suddenly she didn't find Luke to be so funny anymore. "What did you say?" she demanded of him.

Luke spat out the f-word again, then he mocked in a high-pitched tone and a fake lisp, "*Ooooh, thtay away from Joanna! Thee duthn't like that! Get back to work!*"

"Luke, stop," Joanna said, offended not only by the language, but that it was directed toward her closest guy-friend.

"Well, who does he think he is?" Luke went on. He dropped the f-bomb once more and stormed away.

Joanna sighed and rolled her eyes.

Again.

Luke sure was going to be a challenge to figure out.

Well, Luke doesn't like Matthew. Now work is going to be awkward!

Chapter 24: The Last Monday

With only one week left of school, the Liberty High School seniors were preparing for final exams, senior pranks, and of course, graduation. It didn't seem possible to Joanna that in only a few short days, this life of high school that she had known for four years would be behind her.

On Monday morning, she looked at the bustling hallways filled with all her peers. People were talking with each other, grabbing their books, slamming their lockers shut, and rushing to their classrooms. Joanna thought about all her teachers, most of whom she really liked, and how after a few more days, she really wouldn't see them anymore. This time, once the year was over, it would really be *over*.

It would finally be, to quote Mr. Charmin, their "after tomorrow."

Big Ben would no longer dictate the timing of everything Joanna did throughout her day. She would not be back in the fall with a new schedule. She and all the other graduates would be replaced by a new group of leaders in just a few short months. The new seniors would become the distinguished students; Joanna and all her classmates would be *alumni*.

Joanna hadn't really had a chance to get any details from her brother about his break up with Nicole, so when she saw Nicole at her locker Monday morning, Joanna went over to her.

"Hey," Joanna said gently, as Nicole stuffed her backpack into her locker.

Nicole looked up, but then turned back to her bag. "Hi Joanna," she said quietly.

Joanna touched her arm to turn her so that they could face each other. "Are you doing okay?"

"I'm fine." Nicole's reply came too quickly; her tone lacked emotion. She took a deep breath, as if that might boost her confidence. Then she leaned closer to Joanna and said fiercely, "I don't understand what the hell your brother is doing, but I'm not telling anyone about this, and I hope you guys won't either. It's one blasted week before graduation, and I don't need our whole senior class seeing how he has completely ripped my life apart." She pulled out a textbook and slammed her locker shut. "You think he could have waited *one more blasted week*, and not *ruined* what is supposed to be a very momentous time in my life." She started to walk away.

"I'm sorry, Nicole!" Joanna called after her, not knowing what else to say.

Nicole disappeared into the swarm of peers heading to their classes.

"Well, sixth hour ought to be interesting this afternoon," Joanna muttered to herself.

Lisa came up behind Joanna and put her arm happily around her shoulders. "Why will sixth hour be interesting this afternoon?" she asked her.

"Ohhh Lisa," Joanna sighed, resting her head on Lisa's arm. "Christopher broke up with Nicole this weekend…"

Lisa's eyes grew wide. "What?!"

Joanna jumped and quickly covered Lisa's mouth with her hand and looked cautiously all around. "Shhh!" she exclaimed. She leaned close to her ear and said quietly, "It's a long story, but DON'T say anything to anyone. I guess Nicole doesn't want anyone to know."

✳✳✳

Matthew met up with Joanna at her locker before third hour. "Hey," he said.

"Hey."

"This yours?" he asked her, holding a sheet of paper with a drawing on it and some scribbled notes about Beowulf and some other literary figures.

Joanna glanced at it and her face lit up. "Oooh, yes!" She took the paper. "Where'd you find this? I need it for my English Lit exam tomorrow!"

"Charmin said you left it in the room in first hour," he said, referring to their English teacher. The two started walking to their next class – History – together.

"Thank you."

"So, what was going on in the hair accessories aisle yesterday?" Matthew asked her, as they dodged the horde of students trying to get to their classroom quickly.

Joanna just shook her head, so Matthew went on, "Does that bother you, the way he's always cornering you and messin' with you like that? Pokin' you?"

Nobody had to clarify that Matthew was talking about Luke.

Joanna shrugged. "Not really. He's just joking around."

"Well, it doesn't look like it's joking around," Matthew grumbled.

They stopped at the doorway to their classroom and Joanna gently touched Matthew's arm. "Don't worry, Mattie. It's all good." She smiled, and her eyes twinkled. "It's all good," she repeated in a whisper, and then she went into the room and sat in her desk.

***

Joanna caught her brother in the hallway before lunch that morning. "Hey," she said, grabbing his arm as he slammed his locker shut. She leaned close to him and said quietly, "Evidently Nicole doesn't want anyone to know about you breaking up with her..."

"Huh? Well, I suppose not," he said as they started walking down the hall. "She thinks I'm not serious. Or that I'll *realize what I'm doing* and take it all back. But I'm not taking it back. We have to be done. And what's she going to do? Not talk to any of her friends all week? Eventually people are going to find out." The intensity with which Christopher stared straight ahead was ferocious, as though he was determined to not see Joanna's reaction to his insensitivity.

"Well, I know that, but I'm just saying... maybe if it doesn't come up, then don't say anything to anyone this week. She's pretty upset... no sense in making it worse for her."

Christopher stopped and finally looked at his sister, as students brushed by them and the hallway started to clear out. "Joanna, I can't be responsible for how she is responding to this. It's life."

"I *know*." Joanna's tone was agitated and her eyes were pleading. "I'm just saying, try to have some compassion for her this week. It's going to be a tough one for her, and she'd rather not have the whole school know that her life has been completely shattered because you dumped her."

Just be kind, Big Brother!

Christopher rolled his eyes and walked away, but Joanna chased him. "Don't dismiss this!" she advised when she caught up with him. They had fourth hour together, so they both went into the classroom and sat down.

"I'm not the bad guy here," he defended himself. "Don't try to make me the bad guy. You told me not to string her along, but now I'm supposed to go along with her little fantasy for the rest of the week?"

Joanna just looked at him as their classmates joined them and started talking to them. Christopher could see her message perfectly just by the look, in her eyes that matched his own, signaling that he'd better do as she says. Her eyes also signaled that this conversation was done.

Nicole didn't come to lunch that day, and neither did Christopher. Joanna guessed that each of them was avoiding their group lunch so that they wouldn't have to sit together, and she wondered if they would avoid lunch the entire week. The last week of high school. Their last days of lunch together with their friends.

"Don't tell anyone about the break up," Joanna instructed Lisa quickly when the two of them sat down at their lunch table together. Their other friends were still in line or hadn't arrived yet, but she still spoke quietly. "Especially Phebe. Nicole doesn't need to be the center of all her gossip on the last week of school."

"That poor girl," Lisa said compassionately. "How did this happen?"

"I don't know. Christopher told me after Prom that he was ready to move on, and I told him not to drag her on all summer," Joanna confessed to Lisa. She sighed. "I suppose he's been adjusting to the idea in his mind for some time now, whereas she had no clue. The timing on all this just stinks."

Lisa nodded, and a few friends sat down with them.

"Nicole probably went to study hall and Christopher is probably at weight training," Joanna offered confidently when someone commented about them not being there.

Phebe leaned in to Joanna and whispered, "They broke up, didn't they!"

How did she know??!!!

Joanna sighed and whispered back, "DON'T say anything, please!! I'll fill you in later..."

Joanna wondered what pre-calc would be like that afternoon. Her desk was right next to Nicole's, and they always talked and worked together during class. *I guess I'll just walk in like normal and say hello like I always do,* Joanna planned as she navigated the busy hallway to get to the room.

Nicole was already in her seat when Joanna arrived, so Joanna smiled and sat down according to plan. "We missed you at lunch today," she said, forcing her voice to sound upbeat. She hoped to convey to Nicole that she was still part of "the group" and was missed.

But Nicole's response was irritated and cold. "This isn't going to work, Joanna." She turned her body to face the other way and didn't look at Joanna at all the rest of class. When the teacher had the students pair up to do partner work, Joanna was left without her partner as Nicole immediately asked the girl in front of her to work with her.

So, Joanna turned to the only person left near her: Laura Vigent.

Laura. Bland, but safe, Laura.

The review worksheet they were doing was easy, so Joanna spent the entire time analyzing Laura and her worthiness of dating Matthew. If nothing else, this took her mind off of Nicole and the ice bath she had just been doused with. *She's got pretty hair,* Joanna admitted silently in her mind, focusing on Laura now. *If only she'd do something with it. A nice, layered chop would really clean things up.* Then she looked at Laura's hands as Laura pointed to the next equation. *Man hands,* Joanna thought. She looked down at her own hands – her own delicate, long slender fingers with painted nails. Joanna had very pretty, feminine hands. Laura's fingers were blunt and square-like, and Joanna guessed that she was a nail-biter. Laura had a cute body, though. Sort of. *I guess some guys like shorter, curvier girls,* Joanna told herself.

When they finished the worksheet, Joanna asked Laura, "Did you have a good time at Prom? I didn't get to talk to you much that night. Your dress was very pretty."

"Oh, thank you!" Laura beamed. "Yes, I had a great time. Matt is such a nice guy. He was a perfect gentleman."

Matt. He doesn't go by 'Matt,' Laura, Joanna pointed out, again silently inside her head. *His name is <u>Matthew</u>.* She tried to stifle the bitterness that accompanied these thoughts. She thought of Lisa, and how Lisa – always so kind – would handle this conversation. "So, do you like him?" Joanna couldn't help herself. She wanted to get to the bottom of this! "Do you think you guys will go out again?"

"I don't know," Laura replied thoughtfully. "I kind of thought he would have called or something after Prom, but he didn't. We kind of talk in art class still, but nothing that makes me think he wants to do anything again." She paused, and then went on, "You're good buds with him. Has he said anything to you?"

"No," Joanna shook her head. "I mean, I haven't really talked to him much either since Prom night."

"Well, it was nice that you danced with him when he asked you to. I think he kind of wished he would have asked you to go with him. He seems really into you."

This caught Joanna by surprise, and she thought, *Wow! This girl has class!* Realizing that maybe Laura wasn't such a threat after all, Joanna then said sincerely, "Hmmm. Well, I'm glad you had a good time. It was fun having you with us."

***

"So, what's the story with you and Laura?" Joanna asked Matthew bluntly that afternoon as they got into his car after school. They were both scheduled to work that night at the Toy Store, and riding together gave them a quick chance to talk. "You guys goin' out or what?"

"Oh, I don't know," Matthew sighed as he tossed his bag into the back seat of his Toyota Camry. "You wanna grab something to eat before we go to the Store?"

"Yeah, let's go to the sub shop," Joanna said hurriedly, anxious to get back to her original question. The line of cars to get out of the school parking lot seemed endless, but it would go fast. "What do you mean you don't know? Do you like her? You took her to Prom; she seems to like you…"

Obviously, Joanna didn't want Matthew to like Laura, but she needed to find out where this was going if it was indeed going anywhere. And she wanted to appear neutral to the whole idea, to ensure that Matthew would be honest with her.

"I don't know, Jay. She's alright, I guess…"

"But you don't *really* like her, do you," Joanna jumped in, sounding more like she was informing him, instead of asking him. She was always very direct with Matthew.

"I just don't think now is the time to start something. She's going to school in Iowa in the fall, and her family's going to be traveling most of the summer, so it's not like we'd even see each other."

Joanna smiled and looked out the window, relieved.

"Well, what about you?" Matthew asked her then, as they finally turned out of the parking lot. "What's goin' on with Luke?"

"With Luke?" Joanna asked, trying to sound surprised. "What do you mean *with Luke?*"

Matthew wasn't buying it. "C'mon, Jay, don't mess with me. Do you really like this guy? Isn't he a little... not-your-type?"

"Well, what's my type?"

"I don't know... not him!"

"Well, why not him? What's my type?"

"Joanna Marie Conors, you've got the hots for Luke!"

"I never said that!" Joanna defended herself with a half-giggle. "I just asked why he's not my type!"

Matthew kept his eyes on the road but turned his face slightly towards his passenger, affirming, "Because he doesn't seem to be a real winner, Jay. Don't you think you ought to aim a little higher?"

"That's the same thing Christopher says!" she pouted. She looked out the window again.

"Well, your brother is a smart guy. But if you're not going to listen to him, you should at least listen to me."

"So, we flirt a little. Big deal," Joanna said. "It makes work more interesting."

Matthew was quiet for a moment, but then said, "What about Grenzesky? He's still drooling over you, too."

"Yeah, he's kind of creepy," she said, turning serious for a nano-second. "I don't like him." Then she added quickly, "I mean, I like him, as in, he's nice and all, but I don't *like* him-like-him. Like *that.*"

"So, you DO like Luke!" Matthew exclaimed triumphantly.

"Matthew, would you shut up?" Joanna cried with a giggle. "I don't like anybody. Luke is just... weird. He's interesting. I want to figure him out."

"Well, he's not a virgin, just for the record."

Suddenly Joanna's heart rate sped up. "How do you know that?" she asked. Her physical reaction to that statement surprised her... Why should she care if Luke was a virgin or not? Hadn't she already told herself that he wasn't? Why should she care?

"He's bangin' some broad named Shelly who's a complete soap-opera-style mess, and he thinks he's going to *save* her from her messed up self."

"Shelly!" Joanna exclaimed. She had never heard of a Shelly. This couldn't possibly be true. "How do you know this?" she questioned.

"Because he was talking about it in the breakroom the other day. Some loser girl he knows, who's engaged to someone else, but that guy beats her, and she's *trying to get out of the relationship*, supposedly, and Luke is her shoulder to cry on… You know, that whole deal. He was telling Mike and Ken about it."

"Shelly!" Joanna huffed. "Hmmm. Well, I've never heard about a Shelly."

"Well, of course he isn't going to mention this to *you!*" Matthew said logically, stifling a laugh. "He's trying to get it on with you, so he's not going to tell you he's already nailing some other broad!"

"Luke is *not* trying to get it on with me, Matthew. We just like to goof around at work."

"Oh. Okay. Sure. Well, keep it clean, Jay. People are starting to speculate."

"Yes, sir."

Shelly. Hmmm.

What a day... Nicole is a mess about the break up with C. I'm trying to figure out if Matthew likes Laura. He says not really, but I'm not sure. Why do I care if he likes her?

He keeps asking me about Luke. Why does he care if I like Luke?

Do I like Luke??

Matthew told me that Luke is bangin' some chick named Shelly. I have a huge pit in my stomach about this right now. I'll have to do some research on this one.

Chapter 25: Senior Pranks

The last week of school was a whirlwind of exams and senior pranks and a serious extension of spring fever. On Tuesday, Dustin Rollick and some of his buddies collected spare change during lunch from anyone willing to contribute, and they bought a bunch of white mice from the pet store. On Wednesday, they released fifteen little critters in the main hallway right before second hour.

"I missed the whole thing," Phebe said at lunch that day, digging into her taco salad at warped speed. "I was at gym in the field house."

"It was very poorly done," Joanna told her. "Mr. Charmin stepped into the hall immediately, scooped them all up in record time, and took care of it."

"He must have known they were going to do that," Lisa mused. "It seemed too perfect that he just *happened* to be there and just *happened* to be ready to stop it all."

"Yeah, maybe."

Later that morning, two of the senior boys duct-taped an innocent sophomore to the main hall pole. The science teacher rescued him. Then, someone positioned the hall trash can at the top of the stairs by Mrs. Jackson's math classroom. Another boy ran up and kicked the can down the stairs, which left a mess of papers and trash all over the stairwell.

"And you think Luke is immature," Joanna commented to Christopher, when she saw him in the hallway as the trash barrel bounced down the stairs and rolled by them.

"Aw, this is just stupid senior prank stuff," he justified. "It's Senior Prank Day!"

"Seems like a lot of disrespect," she muttered.

"Well, just be glad that Rollick and his crew were willing to provide the entertainment for all of us, so that we don't have to get in trouble," Christopher told her. "I heard a rumor that they're going to be expelled, or not allowed to graduate."

At lunch, Colvin Jaynort sat down with the group and announced, "I'm collecting kisses." He had red lipstick smeared on his cheeks. "I bet Shawn Mercer ten bucks that I could get more smooches on my face than he could by sixth hour." He turned to the girls at the table. "Joanna? Pheebs? Smooch?"

Joanna giggled, and Phebe dug in her purse for a tube of lipstick. "Here," she handed it to Joanna after she put some on her lips. Joanna took it and swiped it across her lips, but only kissed her own fingertips and pressed them gently on Colvin's cheek. Colvin raised his arms up in triumph and cheered, "Woo-hoo! Alright, Lisa? How about you?"

Lisa smiled and said, "Sorry, Jaynort. I promised my kiss to Shawn."

"What?! Traitor!"

On Thursday, unrelated to any of the senior pranks, Joanna and Phebe were walking through the halls between classes, approaching Nathan Hooks' locker. Nathan was there with some buddies, and as soon as they saw the girls coming, they made a big commotion. One kid pretended to bump into Nathan, who then 'dropped' a box of condoms, and the packets scattered all over the floor.

"Aw crap! You effer!" Nathan exclaimed dramatically to his friend. "You made me drop all my stuff!" The boys looked over to be sure Joanna and Phebe were watching, as they scrambled to pick up the little packets.

The girls stopped when they got to the locker. "Ooooh," Phebe sang. She turned to Joanna. "Looks like *someone* wants everyone to *think* he's gonna get some action this weekend!"

Joanna just gave Nathan a look. "Really?" she said, clutching her books close to her chest. Her tone indicated that he was not fooling anyone, that this was just the most ridiculous show she had ever seen.

Nathan ignored her as he scooped up the last packet, and he said to himself, "I need these!"

Joanna and Phebe both rolled their eyes and walked away. "Have you ever!" Phebe muttered disgustedly. "Was that not the biggest show? They totally planned that for when we walked by."

"Oh, I'm Nathan Hooks. And I'm such a man! I want the whole school to know that I'm having sex with Pelin Yilmaz!" Joanna mocked.

Phebe laughed. "Yeah, *I'm Nathan, and I'm such a man now that I'm peelin' the clothes off of Pelin Potatoes!"*

"Whatever. I'm glad I never did anything like that with him," Joanna said.

"Oh my gosh," Phebe agreed. "Can you imagine? He would have broadcasted that throughout the whole school before you would have even gotten your clothes back on!"

"Well, we weren't *that* close to doin' it, Phebe. And I don't think he would be *that* much of a jerk," Joanna said honestly. "But it was a bit of a slippery slope."

Phebe stopped and gently patted Joanna's arm. "Well, you're a smart girl for breaking up with him. That's all that matters. See ya at lunch!" She went into her science classroom. That was one thing about Phebe: her gossipy nature was annoying at times, but the loyalty of her *Freundschaft* to her best friends was something Joanna wouldn't trade for the world.

***

The next time Joanna and Luke were at work, they were assigned to straighten the Lego aisle together at the end of the night. "When do you leave for Germany?" Luke asked her as he pulled a stack of *City Forest Tracker* sets to the front of the shelf.

"Next Monday," Joanna replied. She picked up a box and looked at the price. "How do people even afford these things?" she asked herself. "This *City Fire Station* is a hundred bucks!"

"You gonna send me a postcard?"

"I don't know. Maybe."

"Maybe!"

"Well!" Joanna huffed in a jovial tone. "Why would I need to send you a postcard?" She wanted to see if Luke would say he'd miss her.

He did. "Because I'll miss ya."

"Awwww... You won't even know I'm gone," she challenged him. "You'll be so busy with Shelly, and you'll be working..."

Completely unprepared for that comment, Luke quickly acted like he had no idea who Joanna was talking about. "Shelly?"

"Yeah, your girlfriend," Joanna said casually, pulling another Lego *City Fire*

Station down from the highest shelf to put it on a lower one.

"She's not my girlfriend," Luke said, without questioning now how Joanna might know anything about a person named Shelly.

"Oh, I don't know..." Joanna's tone was playful, and she still did not look at him.

Just then, another co-worker, Liz, came into the aisle with three Lego sets. "Who's not your girlfriend, Luke?" she asked him. Liz was known for jumping right into other people's conversations, a personality quirk that Joanna appreciated at this moment.

"Luke's got a girlfriend named Shelly," Joanna told Liz matter-of-factly, taking the three Lego sets. She put them in their places on the shelves.

"She is not my *girl*friend," Luke corrected her. "She is a *friend.*"

"Oh." Liz shrugged and walked away.

Luke stepped up close to Joanna and said quietly but directly, "She is a *friend.* She is going through some tough stuff right now, and she feels she can talk to me. That's all it is."

Joanna just fake-smiled at him and patted his arm. "Sure, Luke. And I know: You're still a virgin."

So this Shelly person IS real... I kind of trapped Luke tonight at work. I tried to make it like no big deal, but I'm super bothered that there is another girl. Now I obviously can't trust Luke!

167   After Tomorrow

Chapter 26: Graduation

Soon the night of Graduation arrived. Nicole Sheldon cried the entire time, from start to finish, and Joanna wondered if she was emotional about the ceremony, or if she was just plain heartbroken about the break-up with Christopher. Joanna noticed Nicole's parents shooting bitter looks in the direction of the Conors family every so often during the speeches, but Joanna and Christopher stood tall and focused on the event. Joanna regretted that she never got to talk to Nicole that night, which meant she probably would never talk to her again.

The ceremony was lovely. Mr. Charmin gave a speech about the students' *after tomorrow* – about how what has always been their *tomorrow* is now here, it is today! Up until now, *tomorrow* was always just more of the same. But now... now these young adults are prepared for what's next.

"You are all ready now," Mr. Charmin said calmly into the microphone. "You are all ready for what comes *after* this *tomorrow*." His voice rang slow, making his words impactful.

Once the ceremony was done, everyone gathered around the vast lawn in front of the high school to walk around and mingle. Nathan Hooks came up to Joanna and said, "Hey there."

Joanna smiled. "Hey." Then she said with a devilish grin, "Did you get all your rubbers picked up off the floor?"

Nathan chuckled and brought his hand up to his face for a moment. "Yeah... about that. We were just goofin' around. It was Rick's idea."

"You guys need to brush up on your acting skills," Joanna advised with a smile. "But you gave us a good laugh, so thanks for that."

There was a pause, and then Nathan said, "So... this is it, huh?"

"I guess so."

"Graduation always seemed so far away, and suddenly, here it is," he stammered.

Joanna nodded. She looked into Nathan's eyes, and was relieved to realize that she no longer felt sad about their break up. She truly felt nothing for him now, even with his sexy smile, that slightly crooked tooth, and the memories from their time in Hawaii. She had moved on.

"Can I have a hug?" he asked her, opening his arms. As she leaned into his embrace, he said, "This year was a lot of fun. I'm sorry things didn't work out better for us."

Joanna stepped back and took his hands. "It's okay, Nathan. It's like Mr. Charmin said: Our future starts now. Our *tomorrow* is here. No sense in ruminating about the past."

Nathan's eyes grabbed hers. "You take care, okay Joanna? You're a real winner. You're going to make some guy really happy someday. I envy him, whoever he will be."

Joanna hugged him again and said, "Thanks, Nate-dog. You take care too."

Christopher and Joanna finished their good-byes with their teachers and other classmates, and then the Conors family went home. They had a busy weekend ahead of them.

High school is totally done, Herr Journal. Done. No more wandering the halls of Liberty. No more Mr. Charmin. No more worrying about who's cool and who just thinks they're cool. Next up is our grad party, and then all I'll have to worry about is going to Germany. And then college!

After Tomorrow

***

Saturday was Joanna and Christopher's Graduation Open House, and their home was filled with a constant flow of visitors that started early in the afternoon. There were relatives and grandparents and neighbors and friends of the family, friends from school, friends from church, and friends from the Toy Store. The garage was set up with tables and food, and more tables were set up in the backyard under a tent. It was an incredibly lovely day.

At one point, Jodie ran up to her sister and said, "Joanna! Luke and Mike are here from your work!"

Joanna's heart took a little leap, and she darted out to the front of the house. There he was: Luke, with Mike Grenzesky and two other storeroom guys. A few minutes later, Ken also pulled up, with his wife!

"Wow!" Joanna exclaimed when she saw all her work friends. "Who's running the store?"

Ken laughed and said, "When I left this afternoon, we had Deb, Dulcie, and Ned."

"Oh boy!"

The guys went to find Christopher, but Luke stayed with Joanna. He put his arm around her and said, "You look great today."

Joanna leaned into him and smiled. She felt very pretty that day – she was wearing a short sundress and sandals, showing off her long, tanned legs and toned arms. Usually her hair was pulled up into a pony tail at work, but today it was down, with only the sides pinned back.

"I can't believe you came!" she said excitedly.

Joanna and Christopher spent time with each of their guests, and Jodie, Nick, and their parents helped ensure that everyone was welcomed. It was an exhilarating day, and soon the sun was setting. The official hours of their grad party had passed, though many guests remained.

Matthew, Phebe, Lisa, Colvin, and Jodie were all sitting around one table in the garage with the guests of honor, as the evening grew dark. Luke and Mike had been sitting with them too, and when they got up, Luke poked Joanna and said quietly, "Hey, come here."

Mike had gone out to his car for a moment, and Luke said, "We're gonna get going." He gave her a hug and added, "I'm going to miss you."

"Thanks for coming, Luke."

"I really want to give you a good-bye kiss, but Mike would see and then he'd probably kill me."

A good-bye *kiss*!

Joanna's heart took another leap, and suddenly she wished that she and Luke were *anywhere* in the world but at this party! She didn't say anything, and Luke went on just as Mike was walking towards them, "And if *Matthew* ever found out…"

"Here's the card," Mike said when he joined them.

Luke grabbed the envelope from Mike's hand and gave it to Joanna. "Here's your card from us. We wanted you to open it before we leave," he said.

Joanna took the card, but she felt a bit numb. Did Luke really just tell her that he wanted to *kiss* her? She opened the card – on the front, it read, "*Did you ever think this day would come?*" and on the inside, "*We didn't think so either!*" It was signed by both Mike and Luke, and a few other guys from the store. Joanna giggled, but then looked at what was resting loosely inside: thirty Deutsch Marks.

"Oh my goodness, German money!" she exclaimed, overwhelmed by the gesture. Luke and Mike were clearly very proud of their creativity. "You guys are the best," she said, hugging them both at the same time. "Thanks for coming."

✳✳✳

"You guys had quite a turnout!" Mrs. Conors exclaimed to her children late that evening, as she added some dishes to the dishwasher. It was almost midnight, and the last of the guests had finally left.

"I can't believe how late people stayed," Christopher commented.

"Today was so fun…" Joanna said wistfully. She set the basket filled with cards on the kitchen table.

"Who *were* all those people?" Nick asked, reaching for a can of Coke from the cooler that had been wheeled to the doorway.

"Ah-ah-ah! No more pop!" Mrs. Conors stopped her son before he pulled the tab on the can. "Put that back, Nicholas!"

"Awwww!" Nick whined.

"I *know*," Mr. Conors agreed, referring to Nick's original question. "I was beginning to wonder who all those people were! I figured some of them just showed up because they saw a party." He grabbed another trash bag from under the sink and went back out to the garage.

"We don't need to invite all those people when we have my party," Jodie informed her mother. "Like, who were those two old people that came with Grandma and Grandpa Shermack? That woman stared at me the whole time, and kept saying Congratulations to *me*!"

Mrs. Conors smiled. "Oh, Great-Uncle Bernie and Great-Aunt Sylvia. Grandma really wanted to bring them for some reason."

"Well, they don't have to come to mine in two years," Jodie reiterated.

"They'll probably be dead by then," Nick offered. "They looked like they were about three hundred years old." He started to giggle at his own joke.

Mrs. Conors whacked her son gently on his head with her dish towel and said, "Never mind, young man. You get to bed."

Mr. Conors came back in with a crock pot, and when he set it down, Joanna went over to her parents. She wrapped her arms around both of them and said, "Thank you, Mom and Dad, for being the best parents ever, and for giving us this great party. I had such a fun day. Actually, I've had such a fun life, thanks to you."

"Aww!" Mrs. Conors smiled and looked at her husband. "I think that's the nicest thing she's ever said to us!"

"Well, it's easy to be 'good parents' when you've got good kids," Mr. Conors acknowledged, kissing his daughter on the top of her head. He reached over to Christopher and patted his son on the shoulder. "We are extremely proud of both of you. I couldn't be a prouder dad than I am right now."

***

That night, as Joanna lay in bed, many thoughts were racing through her mind. Her life in high school was officially done. Her life in America was temporarily done; she was all packed and ready for the airport in the morning. Her sadness about breaking up with Nathan Hooks was officially gone. She liked high school, but she didn't really think she'd miss it too much after all. She was excited about Germany. She was excited about the rest of her summer after Germany, working at the Toy Store… and working with Luke.

Luke. He said he wished he could kiss her! And now she would be leaving for a month!

Black-Cat-Black strolled up to her with his loud purr and plopped down on her pillow. Joanna grabbed her journal and quickly wrote,

C & I are leaving for Germany soon. I think I really, really like Luke. I'm going to miss Phebe and Lisa and Matthew and Jodie and Nick… And I'm going to miss Luke.

She carefully placed her journal in her carry-on bag, on the floor near her dresser. Then she crawled back into bed and fell asleep.

About the Author

Amy (Schire) Gleason grew up in St. Paul, Minnesota, and started developing her Woodland Hills characters when she was just ten years old. Her first books were about Joanna, Christopher, Matthew, Lisa, and Phebe as children, and their adventures took place at their school, in their homes, and in their community. Those adventures remained only as drafts, locked away in the author's archives, but the young Ms. Schire continued to write throughout her high school and college years. Here she found more inspiration for her characters to be young adults, rather than children, and the Woodland Hills Novel Series was born. These storylines evolved over the next thirty years, each book enduring countless revisions, until they became the finished copies that you hold in your hands today.

Amy Gleason lives with her husband and two daughters in Stillwater, Minnesota. She is always writing, but she also enjoys running, biking, teaching, scrapbooking, and traveling.

What's next?

Stay up-to-date with the Woodland Hills novel series! Scan to view all info about Woodland Hills and author Amy Gleason at www.amygleason.net.

Contact Information:

website: www.amygleason.net

email: amyschiregleason@gmail.com

orders: store.bookbaby.com